Heads Up!

Heads Up!

Dawn Hunter
and Karen Hunter

James Lorimer & Company Ltd., Publishers
Toronto, 2001

First publication in the United States, 2001

James Lorimer & Company Ltd. acknowledges the support of the Ontario Arts Council for our publishing program. We acknowledge the support of the Government of Canada through the Book Publishing Industry Development Program (BPIDP) for our publishing activities. We acknowledge the support of the Canada Council for the Arts for our publishing program.

Cover illustration: Sharif Tarabay

Cataloguing in Publication Data

Hunter, Dawn
  Heads up!

(Sports stories; 44)
ISBN 1-55028-719-2 (bound)   ISBN 1-55028-718-4 (pbk.)

I. Hunter, Karen, 1960–   . II. Title. III. Series: Sports stories (Toronto, Ont.); 44.

PS8565.U57845H42 2000   jC813'.54   C00-931909-3
PZ7.H86He 2000

James Lorimer & Company Ltd.,   Distributed in the United States by:
Publishers   Orca Book Publishers
35 Britain Street   P.O. Box 468
Toronto, Ontario   Custer, WA USA
M5A 1R7   98240–0468

Printed and bound in Canada.

Contents

To Mum, Dad, and Jean,
for keeping the Boy Wonder occupied,
and to Scott and his friends,
for the inspiration.

1

Starting Out

He shoots. G-o-o-a-a-l!" Glen yelled as his friend Jacob kicked his hackeysack through the space between the concrete bumper blocks in the school parking lot. It was a beautiful, warm September afternoon, and Glen and Jacob were in no hurry to head home.

"Lucky shot," Glen teased, pushing his friend's shoulder and scooping up the footbag before Jacob could reach it. He bounced it a few times on his knee but couldn't control it, and Jacob snatched it as it fell.

The two boys were looking forward to playing soccer on the same house league team this year at their school, William Burgess Elementary. Both boys hoped to earn a position on the final team, which would represent the school in a one-day tournament against teams from seven other local schools.

"Skill, man, it's all skill," Jacob laughed, demonstrating his fancy footwork once again. "Listen, I had to put up with you all summer thinking you were Mr. Baseball. Now you're on my turf." Jacob dropped his voice, imitating the smooth tones of a sports announcer. "Welcome to soccer 101."

"You wish!" Glen replied, throwing the hackeysack playfully at his friend. Grinning, Jacob ducked quickly, and the footbag went sailing over his head into the school yard.

"Hey!" Jacob called to a husky, dark-haired boy who was walking across the field. "Can you toss that back, please?"

The boy sauntered over and picked up the footbag. Rather than just throwing it back, he began to bounce it from knee to knee, keeping it from dropping. As Glen and Jacob watched, he began to walk towards them, still bouncing the footbag. He deftly moved it from his knees to the insides of his feet and finally kicked it straight to Glen when he was closer to them.

"Wow!" Glen exclaimed. "Those were some cool moves, man."

Jacob nodded in agreement.

"Thanks." The older boy smiled smugly. "It was nothing. I used to play with a footbag all the time when I was first learning some soccer skills. But I really don't need it now."

Jacob raised his eyebrows. "Well, it's still a good way to stay sharp. And besides, it's fun."

The other boy shrugged. "Whatever."

"I'm Glen Thomson, and this is Jacob Collins," Glen said, pointing to his best friend. "We are both in grade five here. Do you go to this school too?"

"Yeah, but I'm in grade six. My name is Danny Jackson." He took out a pack of gum and pushed out a few pieces. He put the package away without offering any to the other boys. "Are you guys playing soccer this year?" Danny asked, popping the gum into his mouth.

"Yeah, we both are." Jacob reached over and took his footbag back from Glen. "You?"

"Of course! I was the best player on the team at the soccer camp I went to this summer. Which team are you on?" Danny asked, turning to Glen.

"We are both on Mr. Masotti's team," Glen replied.

"You're kidding! So am I. That means that I can help you guys out." Danny grinned.

Jacob rolled his eyes.

"Sure, that would great!" Glen exclaimed. "This is my first year playing soccer, but Jacob is already pretty good. His dad has been teaching him his whole life."

"Oh. Well, I'm sure I can still teach you something new," Danny said, barely glancing at Jacob. "I gotta get going. I'll see you guys at practice." He strode away, whistling, and hopped onto an expensive-looking mountain bike. As he watched Danny leave, Glen saw that the other boy had his dark hair pulled back into a small ponytail. Glen had thought Danny's hair was short, but the ponytail was kind of cool.

"Man! What an attitude," Jacob said as soon as Danny was out of earshot. "'I'm sure I can still teach you something new,'" Jacob said, mimicking Danny's arrogant tone.

"But he really was good with that footbag," Glen protested. "Maybe you already know it all, but I don't. I think he's okay. Come on," he said, looking at his watch. "Let's get going."

"I can't believe our first game is this Wednesday." Jacob hoisted his backpack onto his shoulder. "I wonder what it'll be like having girls on our team?"

"Hey, as long as they can pass the ball and shoot, I don't care if we play with aliens!" Glen pulled off his baseball cap and flicked his blond hair out of his eyes. He glanced at the East York Eagles crest before putting the hat back on, thinking about the summer and wishing he had done certain things differently. He promised himself that things would be different on the soccer team. "At least we get to practise tomorrow."

Leaving the school yard and crossing Woodville Avenue, the boys headed home.

"I guess your dad is pretty happy that you're playing soccer, eh?" Glen asked.

"Oh, yeah." Jacob's dad had come to most of the boys' baseball games in the summer, but he was always asking them why they didn't play soccer instead. "Maybe now he'll stop telling those stories of 'When I was a child in Barbados, everyone played soccer.'"

Glen laughed. "I'm glad Andrew doesn't make me listen to those kinds of stories." Glen's stepfather and mother had only been married for a year, and he and Andrew were still trying to build a relationship. "But playing house league games right after school means most parents won't be able to come to them anyway."

"I just hope we both make it onto the final team," Jacob said as they turned onto Hassard Avenue. "What did Coach Masotti say about how the team is chosen?"

"I think he said we play each of the other teams in the school, then the coaches get together and choose the final team for the big tournament."

"It would be so cool to win the trophy." Jacob lifted an imaginary trophy high in the air.

"Tell me, Big J, how does it feel to be the best soccer player in Toronto?" Glen said, grabbing the ruler out of his backpack to use as a microphone.

"It feels great! I'd like to thank my parents and all the fans out there for making it a great season!"

"Come on," Glen laughed, shoving the ruler into his pack again. "The light's green. I'll race you the rest of the way home!"

Jacob caught up to Glen outside Glen's house.

"I win!" Glen panted, holding onto the stair railing.

"Ah, you cheated," Jacob teased. "Anyway, I gotta get home. I'll see you tomorrow."

Jacob headed up the street towards his house as Glen bounded up the front steps of his house, and unlocked the front door. "Mom?" he called as he dropped his backpack and baseball cap onto the couch and went into the kitchen at the back of the house. Taking a glass from the cupboard above the sink, he poured a big glass of apple juice and saw his mother in the backyard.

Sliding open the screen door, Glen stepped out onto the deck and over Jasper, the family's yellow Lab, and sat down on the steps.

"Hey, there you are," Catherine said, standing up and brushing the dirt from her jeans. "Whew! Another couple of weeks and I won't have to worry about these weeds anymore." She shook off her gardening gloves and tightened the scarf holding back her thick blond curls. "How was school?" she asked, plunking herself down beside Glen and taking a sip of his juice.

"It was pretty good, actually. The soccer teams were posted, and Jacob and I are on the same team."

"Great! Do you know many of the other kids on the team?"

"I know most of the grade fives, but only a few of the grade sixes." Glen paused to drain his glass. "Jacob and I met a new guy named Danny as we were leaving school today. I guess I'll meet the rest of the team at practice tomorrow morning."

"Just remember that it's only for fun," his mother warned. "Don't get too caught up in the competition."

"I won't. Where's Megan?" he asked, changing the subject. He had grown quite fond of his younger stepsister and usually helped her with her homework after school.

"She's at her friend's house today," his mom said, staring at the nearby flowerbed. "I wanted to have a little time alone to talk to you."

Glen frowned, wondering why his mother sounded so serious. He hoped they weren't moving.

"Your dad called earlier," she began.

Glen's heart leapt, as it always did when his father was mentioned. No matter how many times his dad had broken promises, Glen always hoped that the next time would be different. He forced himself to keep quiet and let his mother finish.

Catherine put her hand on Glen's shoulder. "Your dad's company has transferred him out of the California office and back to Toronto. He arrives this week."

Glen's stomach was suddenly full of butterflies. He couldn't believe his ears. The questions began pouring out.

"Where's he staying? Is it a permanent transfer? When can I see him? What—"

"Wait a second," Catherine interrupted gently. "Give me a chance to answer. He's going to be staying at the King Eddie hotel until he can find a place to live. He said that he'll probably buy a condo downtown. As far as he knows, it's permanent, but he thought California was, too. He asked whether you and Josh wanted to see him on Sunday."

"Even if Josh doesn't want to go, I sure do!" He couldn't wait until his older brother got home. "Can I tell Josh when he gets in?"

"I've already told Josh, and he's agreed to go with you on Sunday." Catherine reached over and smoothed Glen's hair, which was still ruffled from his baseball cap. "You know that Josh may not be as excited about this as you are. And you know how important your dad's work is to him. He'll be really busy for the first few months. You might not be able to see him as much as you would like."

Glen pulled his head away from his mother's hand. "It might be different when he's living here," he mumbled, playing with his shoelaces.

Catherine sighed and dropped her hands into her lap. "I do hope it is different this time. I know it was hard on you when he cancelled his trip to see you and Josh this summer."

Glen shrugged. "I was kinda mad at him. But the last time he called, he said he was sorry, and we talked about it a little. I'm okay about the summer now."

Inside Glen wasn't so sure. He didn't want his mother to worry about him, but it was hard to forget how awful he had felt when his dad had let him down.

Catherine looked at Glen silently for a moment. "Well, I'm glad that you are looking forward to seeing him. I just don't want to see you get hurt again."

Glen smiled at his mom. "It's okay. I think I'll go upstairs and start my homework now," he said, standing up.

"Sure." Catherine picked up the empty juice glass and headed inside with Glen. "Just be sure to come and set the table for dinner in an hour."

"Jasper!" Glen called. "Come on, boy. Let's go upstairs."

Jasper was a present from Glen's father just before his dad had moved to California, and Glen often shared his feelings with the dog. No matter what Glen said, Jasper wouldn't tell a soul.

Glen didn't really have any homework to do, and he felt a little bad about not being straight with his mother. He really just wanted some time to sort out his feelings and think about what it would mean to have his dad living so close again.

"I wonder when Josh will be home?" Glen said aloud, petting Jasper, who had jumped up on the bed. "It's too bad he had to work after school, today of all days."

Glen settled himself against the headboard, with Jasper's head resting on his lap. He stroked the dog's silky ears and Jasper sighed contentedly.

"You know, Jasper, I'm not sure what I'm feeling anymore. When my mom first told me that Dad would be coming back, I was so excited because I haven't seen him in so long. But I can't help thinking about all the other times when I was excited and he let me down. I really hope things will be different. I do miss him, and I hope Josh will chill out a little. He said some harsh things about dad in the summer. What do you think, boy? Will it be better this time?"

Jasper licked Glen's hand as if in agreement. Glen laughed and wrapped his arms around Jasper, hoping he was right.

2

Teamwork

"All right," Coach Masotti called, "everyone on the field doing the warmup stretches I showed you at yesterday's practice. Grab a partner to work with."

Glen and Jacob paired up automatically. Glen saw Danny coming towards them, but he veered when he saw Glen and Jacob standing together. Scott Mekler, who was also in grade six, approached Danny. Scott was a friendly, quiet boy, whose ready smile showed off his dimples.

Danny and Scott sat down near Glen and Jacob, and the boys faced their partners with their legs outstretched in a V and the soles of their shoes touching. They reached forward and clasped each other's wrists. Then each boy took turns leaning forward as far as they could while the other pulled gently.

"Hey, I talked to my dad last night," Glen said as he stretched towards Jacob. "We're definitely going out for lunch on Sunday."

"Is Josh gonna go?" his friend asked.

When Glen's brother had gotten home from work on Monday, the two had spoken briefly about their dad's return. Glen knew the way Josh felt about their father and his unreliability. At seventeen Josh was six years older than Glen, and when their dad had cancelled his plans to visit in the summer, Josh had reminded Glen that his own memories of their family before their parents had divorced were much clearer. When Bob and Catherine were married, Bob had spent little time with his sons because he was away on business so often. Catherine had tried to protect the boys from disappointment when she could, but Josh had been old enough to see what was really going on. He told Glen that he couldn't help resenting his father even though he still loved him. Glen knew that Josh was having trouble dealing with those feelings, but maybe they could make a fresh start at lunch.

"Yeah, he said he would, but I think my mom is making him go," Glen sighed. "I really wish Josh would lighten up and give my dad a chance."

The boys shifted positions and each folded their left leg so that the bottom of their foot rested against the inside of their right thigh. Reaching their arms along the outstretched leg, they tried to touch their toes.

"Hey, don't push too far," Coach Masotti said, walking around and helping some of the kids. "It shouldn't hurt. You just want to stretch out those muscles so that you don't injure them in the game."

Angelo Masotti reminded Glen of a small bear, with his sturdy square frame and neatly trimmed black beard and moustache. He taught grade six and coached several of the house league soccer teams. Coach Masotti was an athlete himself and taught the kids how to avoid injuries through warmups and stretching. Glen liked him and hoped that he might have him as a teacher next year.

"Listen to that guy," Jacob whispered to Glen.

"Who? Danny?" Glen kept his voice low.

"Yeah! He's telling Scott about soccer camp and all the same stuff he told us on Monday."

"Okay everyone, gather round," the coach called, waving them over to the sidelines and ending Glen and Jacob's conversation. "Soccer is truly a game of teamwork. You have to work together to move the ball up the field and score the goals. Defenders, halfbacks, and strikers each have to know where they should be on the field and when to pass the ball to stay in position. We play fifteen-minute halves, with ten minutes in between.

"We will only be playing once a week for five weeks, and then we'll be choosing the final team to represent the school at the playoff tournament. We'll talk more about the tournament as we get closer to it. For now, you need to know that players will be chosen for the final team for their ability to play as team members as much as for their skills on the field."

The coach proceeded to assign positions. The kids would get to try each position, but they would start the games in their assigned spots. Their team had fifteen players, and eleven were on the field at any one time. Glen would start as a defender, and his job would be to defend the goal. Glen's skills in passing and dribbling were not as strong as some of the other player's skills, but he had a good team sense and was able to stay goal-side of the player he was marking. His height was also an advantage, since he was taller than most of the other kids. He wouldn't be starting the game, but would rotate in later.

Jacob would play as a halfback, which was like a quarterback, setting up the offence. Jacob seemed to have a natural ability with a soccer ball and was able to make the short, sharp precision passes needed in the overlapping offence style of play, and he would start the game.

Kaitlynn Sathi was one of the six girls on the team and she always had her straight black hair pulled back tightly into a ponytail. When the coach announced that she would be one of the goalkeepers, Glen saw a big smile light up her face. Glen had watched her at practice, and he thought she would be a great goalkeeper. She was tall, which gave her more reach to grab the ball, and she was light on her feet. During practice, few balls had gotten past her.

"If I had known there would be girls on our team, I might not have signed up." Glen jumped as Danny whispered in his ear. He hadn't realized that Danny was standing right behind him.

"Hey, the girls play better than I do!" Glen laughed. "I think Kaitlynn will be a great goalie."

"Dylan Messner," Coach Masotti said, "you'll be a defender too."

Dylan smiled at Glen. The two boys were in the same class, but didn't know each other very well. Dylan was almost as tall as Glen, but was a little more muscular. He seemed friendly, and during the first practice, Glen had noticed what a good player Dylan was. Since they were playing the same position, he hoped he could learn a few things from the other boy.

Scott and Danny would both be strikers, responsible for most of the shooting for the team. Danny would start the game and Scott would sub in later.

Coach Masotti announced the rest of the starting lineup and the positions they would play. With fifteen kids on the team, four would sit at any one time, and eleven would play. The team had named itself the Tigers.

This first game was against the Spiders, and Scott went to take the coin toss for home side.

"Heads!" he shouted as the coin was flipped.

"Tails!" the other coach, Mrs. Deroy, announced as the coin landed. The Spiders would wear orange vests over their T-shirts since uniforms were not used in house league games. The Tigers would just wear their shorts and T-shirts.

Both coaches would ref the game, and Coach Masotti placed the ball at centre field. The teams lined up on either side of the half line and the Spiders kicked off.

Scott and Glen sat down together on the sidelines. Glen looked around the field and was surprised to see quite a few kids from the school watching the game from the sidelines and cheering on each team.

The action on the field was fast paced, and Glen was happy to see that their team was playing so well together. He couldn't wait to get out there. The Tigers were doing a great job of defending their own goal and moving the play upfield towards the Spiders' net.

Suddenly, one of the Spiders' halfbacks took possession of the ball from the Tigers. She moved like lightening, dribbling the ball out of reach of the nearest Tiger players.

"Sharon! I'm open!" one of the Spiders' strikers yelled, waving his arms and running towards the goal.

Dylan ran after him, frantically trying to get back into position and goal-side. Sharon sent a flick pass straight to her striker, and he trapped it easily.

"Stay with him, Dylan!" Glen and Scott were both shouting excitedly from the sidelines. Glen could hear the Spiders yelling "Go! Run! Faster!" from the other side of the field.

The striker faked a shot to the left, and Dylan hurtled himself in that direction, trying to block the shot. The fake worked perfectly and the striker took the ball to the right, around Dylan.

Glen could hardly contain himself and was jumping up and down on the sidelines. "Come on, Kaitlynn! You can do it!"

He watched as Kaitlynn tensed and began shuffling her feet along the goal line, trying to read the direction the shot would take. She crouched, ready to spring, never taking her eyes off the ball.

The striker drew his leg back and used the laces to send the ball screaming at the right side of the net. Kaitlynn launched herself to the right, stretching her arms out and grabbing the ball into her chest at the last second.

The Tigers were all whooping and clapping at the amazing save.

"Wow! That was awesome!" Scott exclaimed. "Looks like Kaitlynn will be a great goalie!"

"I know what you mean," Glen agreed. "She was right on the mark for that one."

Kaitlynn looked for an open teammate and threw the ball back into play, but Alex missed the pass and the Spiders took possession.

The Spiders scurried downfield, passing the ball and trying to get into scoring position. Just past the midfield mark, Glen saw Jacob move in to tackle. Jacob was closest to the player with possession of the ball. He challenged the Spider by keeping his body low and his weight forward, staying between the attacker and the Tiger net.

Jacob moved quickly but kept himself under control, forcing the attacking player to the outside, away from the net. Jacob glanced over his shoulder to see Danny backing him up, in case the attacker got away from Jacob.

Glen held his breath as Jacob stepped in as close as possible to the other player, using his other foot to make contact with ball. He moved into the Spider's space and kept his weight moving through with the ball. He used his shoulder to take the weight of the other player and shield the ball from him. One touch was all it took to knock the ball loose. Jacob moved after it and touched it again to gain possession.

Glen watched Danny race upfield, past Jacob, and close to the net. Glen noticed that Danny was a fast runner, even though he was big and stocky. Danny began yelling to Jacob, signalling that he had a clear shot. Jacob chipped the ball to Danny, who trapped it and pivoted in one fluid motion. He sent the ball flying, straight into the upper corner, leaving the Spider goalkeeper frozen in a crouch.

"Way to go, Jacob and Danny!" Glen yelled, as he and the other subs jumped to their feet, cheering.

"Great work, guys!" Coach Masotti called. "All right — Glen you're in for Dylan, and Scott, you're in for Sapna."

Glen sprinted onto the field and lined up between Jacob and Danny for the Spiders to kick off again. The ball came straight to Glen and he quickly passed it off to Jacob, falling back into the defender's position. He watched Jacob move the ball up the field and was impressed by how well he controlled the ball. Then, on a push pass, a Spiders' striker intercepted the ball.

The momentum of the game had carried most of the Tigers up the field, leaving only Glen and one other defender between the Spiders and Kaitlynn. Glen's heart started to pound as the striker moved towards him. Remembering what Jacob had done, Glen tried to tackle, but lost his balance and staggered, leaving the ball in the striker's possession. But his teammate had been covering the play, and kicked it out of the goal area, sending it almost to the halfway line, where the rest of the team were now in position.

Twweett! The coach's whistle shrilled, ending the first half of the game.

The players ran to the sidelines and gathered around the coach. Some kids pulled bottles of water out of their backpacks.

"That was a great way to start the game!" Coach Masotti glanced at his clipboard. "Danny, you and Jacob will be sitting to start the last half, and Scott and Alex will start."

"But, Coach, just let me finish the game!" Danny protested.

"No, Danny," the coach said, turning around. "You have played the whole game so far. You did really well, so enjoy the rest and let someone else have a turn."

Danny folded his arms across his chest, and glared at the back of the coach's head.

Coach Masotti gave the usual halftime pep talk and offered each player a few pointers. With two minutes left before the game started, Glen and Jacob grabbed a few seconds to talk about the team.

"Hey, you really *are* a good player," Glen admitted. "I thought you might have just been bragging."

"Thanks, man." Jacob flashed a smile. "There are a few good players on our team. Looks like Danny won't be the only star."

"Scott's in his class." Glen dropped his voice. "He told me that Danny just moved here in the summer. Scott heard that his family is rich, but that Danny was caught shoplifting."

Jacob raised his eyebrows in surprise. "Oh, yeah? He does look kinda tough."

"Did you see the mountain bike he was riding yesterday? It's gotta be a thousand bucks at least." Glen couldn't keep the admiration out of his voice. He looked over at Danny, who was standing a little apart from the team with his back to them.

Coach Masotti called the team into a huddle, and they all placed their hands on top of each other's in the centre of the circle. "G-o-o-o Tigers!" they yelled, pulling their hands out and up over their heads as the Spiders did the same thing on the other side of the field.

The coaches called for the kickoff. The second half of the game was much slower, with lots of give and take between the teams. Both teams fought hard, but neither scored another goal, giving the Tigers the victory. The players lined up at the halfway line and shook hands.

Afterwards, Danny stayed on the field bouncing his own soccer ball on his knees and feet without letting it touch the ground. Glen and Jacob stopped to watch.

"Wow! How long can you keep doing that?" Glen asked.

"Aw, I could do this for hours." Danny shrugged, never taking his eyes off the ball.

"I would have dropped it by now, for sure."

"Well, at the soccer camp I went to in the summer, we used to have contests, and I always won." Danny flipped the ball expertly to Glen, who caught it, and the boys all walked off the field together.

As they gathered their things, an expensive-looking silver SUV pulled into the parking lot.

"Hey, there's my dad," Danny said, waving. "Where do you live, Glen?"

"Oh, over on Beechwood, and Jacob lives up the street from me."

"I'm on Hopedale, so I'm sure my dad will drive you home. You can come too, I guess," Danny said, turning to Jacob.

The boys jogged over to the parking lot, and they all piled into the back of the SUV. Danny introduced them to his dad and asked his dad to drop them off at home, since they lived so close to Danny.

"Sure, no problem," Mr. Jackson replied. "Seat belts, everyone."

"Wow! This sport ute is really cool! Is that GLE tracking?" Glen asked, pointing to the system in the front.

"Sure is. My dad only buys the best. My mom's got one too, but it's red. What kind of car does your dad drive, Glen?" Danny asked smugly.

"Well, my dad's moving back from California this weekend, and I'm sure that he'll get something like this. Maybe he'll get the one where you can show movies in the back and stuff."

The two boys continued chatting, and Glen noticed that Jacob wasn't saying much as he looked out the window.

Mr. Jackson pulled up in front of Jacob's house.

"Thanks for the ride home, Mr. Jackson," Jacob said, opening the door and pulling his backpack off the seat. "I'll see you tomorrow, Glen. Good game, Danny," he added quietly.

"What's his problem anyway?" Danny asked as soon as the door was shut.

"What do you mean?" Glen said, wrinkling his forehead.

"Well, he hardly said a word on the way home. He seems kinda stuck up."

"Who, Jacob?" Glen asked incredulously. "No way. Jacob's a good guy. We've been best friends for years now. He was the first guy I met when I moved here. He might be a little shy, but he's not stuck up."

Danny tilted his head to the side and raised one eyebrow. "Whatever. Hey, do you wanna eat lunch together sometime?" he asked.

"Sure. Jacob and I usually eat at school, and you can join us anytime."

Danny nodded, but Glen thought he seemed a little put off. As Mr. Jackson stopped outside Glen's house, Glen thanked him for the ride and closed the door, happy that he seemed to have made a new friend.

3

High Hopes

Hurry up, Glen!" Josh called, as he stood at the bottom of the stairs. "We're meeting dad for lunch, not dinner."

Upstairs, Glen stood in front of the mirror in his room, wondering whether he should change his shirt and trying to comb his blond hair back off his face. The butterflies in his stomach had kept him from eating breakfast, and he could hear it rumbling now.

"I'm coming, I'm coming," he answered. He gathered up a few photographs from the summer to show his dad and ran down the stairs. The day was overcast and cool, so he stopped to grab his jacket on his way out the door.

Since it was Sunday, the buses ran less frequently, so Catherine was driving the boys to Broadview subway station. She was on her way to work that day at the small café she owned on the Danforth. From there, Glen and Josh would catch the subway west to Bloor station, and then transfer south to King. Bob was staying at the King Edward, a luxurious hotel downtown.

Stopping outside the subway station, Catherine gave Glen a quick kiss on the cheek. "Just try to take the day as it comes," she said softly. "Josh, keep an eye on Glen. And don't forget that you promised me you would give your dad a chance."

"Yes, Mother," Josh sighed, rolling his blue eyes as he shut the car door. The wind ruffled his blond hair, and he pulled his jacket tighter around his thin frame.

The boys settled themselves into their seats on the subway. Josh slouched down with his arms folded across his chest. Being six feet tall, he had to tuck his long legs under the seat to let people walk by. Glen perched on the edge of his seat, and couldn't stop jiggling his leg up and down.

"I can't believe it's been over a year since we saw Dad," Glen blurted.

"Yeah, he probably won't even recognize us," Josh said sarcastically.

Glen frowned. "Josh, stop it. You said you wouldn't go there. You're gonna wreck the whole day!" he exclaimed, his face turning red.

Josh's expression softened. "I'm sorry, Glen. I just get frustrated with Dad sometimes. For your sake I'll try to watch what I say."

The brothers were quiet for the rest of the trip, each caught up in his own thoughts.

Arriving at the hotel, the doorman nodded to them. Glen was a little awed by the hotel lobby. He looked around, staring up at the carvings along the two-storey-high ceiling. He wandered across the thick rugs to touch the palm trees and run his hand down the cool marble pillars.

Glen elbowed Josh as he suddenly spotted his dad sitting in an inviting brown leather armchair.

"There he is," Glen whispered.

Glen couldn't help noticing that his dad had changed since he last saw him. As usual he was well dressed. His khaki trousers had a crisp crease running down each pant leg. His brown loafers were gleaming, and his light blue shirt looked freshly ironed. However, Glen thought that under the California tan, his dad looked tired and thinner.

"Dad!" Glen waved excitedly. He saw a smile break across his father's face as he stood up and walked towards them carrying a shopping bag from Eddy Bauer.

Glen ran the last few feet to his dad and grabbed him tightly in a hug.

"Hey, Sport, it's so good to see you! I really missed you guys."

"I missed you too, Dad," Glen said, stepping aside as Josh slowly walked up beside them.

As Bob moved to hug Josh, Josh took half a step backwards and stuck out his hand instead.

Glen saw the look of surprise on his dad's face as he hesitated for a moment before clasping Josh's hand.

"Good to see you, Josh," he said cautiously.

"You too." Josh nodded his head curtly.

"Well," Bob said, turning back to Glen, "are you guys hungry? I thought we could stay in the hotel and grab brunch over in Café Victoria." Bob slung an arm around Glen's shoulder as they walked to the restaurant.

Glen's dad requested a table in the far corner where fewer people were seated. The room was large, with dozens of tables covered with white tablecloths and fresh flowers in the centre of each. With its trellised walls and greenery, the café reminded Glen of an outdoor gazebo.

Sitting down at the table, the boys made small talk with their dad while they ordered their food and waited for it to arrive.

"I have something for each of you." Bob reached into the bag he had set beside his chair. He pulled out two brightly wrapped packages and handed one to Glen and one to Josh.

"Wow, Dad! Thanks! But I didn't get you anything," Glen said, scooping up the package and shaking it.

"I don't need presents, Glen. It's enough for me to finally see you boys again."

"Well, if you had come up in the summer…" Josh mumbled.

Glen shot a furious look at his brother and kicked him under the table.

Bob stared at Josh. As Bob started to speak, Glen ripped open the wrapping paper noisily.

"I wonder what this could be?" he said before his dad could get a word out, hoping to ease the tension. "Awesome! A Glovesmith baseball glove! I saw their Web site on the Internet, and they make these by hand. Thanks! I'm sure it'll be great next summer. I'm playing soccer right now."

Glen thought his dad looked a little disappointed. "Hey, maybe we can play catch this fall and break it in," he hurried to add.

"I'm sure we can," Bob said, smiling. "Are you going to open yours, Josh?"

Silently, Josh opened his package and pulled out a black leather backpack.

"I thought you could use it when you go to university next year."

"Yeah, it's great. Thanks." Josh nodded.

"This is so soft," Glen said, reaching over to touch the backpack.

The waiter appeared and set their meals down in front of them, and they ate in silence for few minutes.

"So, what universities have you applied to, Josh?" Bob said, turning to his older son.

"None. It's too early to start applying," Josh answered abruptly.

"It's never too early. What about early acceptance?" Bob demanded.

Glen closed his eyes as he heard that familiar tone in his father's voice. He knew that this kind of conversation between his dad and his brother always ended in an argument. Opening his eyes, he watched Josh stiffen in his chair and could see the muscles in his brother's jaw tightening.

Josh stabbed at his food with his fork, heaving a sigh and staring at a point just beyond his father's shoulder. Glen knew that his dad hated it when someone wouldn't meet his eyes. Josh knew it too.

Bob launched into a speech about the importance of a good education, and that choosing the right university could make or break a career. Glen's mouth dropped open in horror when Josh suggested that perhaps he wouldn't be going to university at all. He knew Josh was just trying to get a rise out of their dad. Bob was a bit of a snob when it came to education.

Glen saw his dad's eyes widen and his face turn red. Suddenly, Bob squinted at Josh and nodded his head.

"Okay, Josh. I know what you're doing. Just remember that you'll never get anywhere in life by being a smart aleck." Glen saw the exasperation in his dad's face as he reached up under his glasses and rubbed the bridge of his nose.

"Hey, how's Jasper these days?" Bob asked, looking at Glen. "He must be getting pretty big by now."

"Well, yeah, he's almost four."

"My gosh, it's been four years already?"

"Yeah, time sure flies, doesn't it, Dad?" Josh added, glancing at his watch.

Glen nervously toyed with his food. He was having trouble swallowing anything. He could almost feel the tension at the table and couldn't stop the words from tumbling out to fill each silence.

As the waiter came to clear the plates, Josh looked at his watch again.

"Look, Dad, we really have to get going. I have to work this afternoon, and I have to get Glen home first."

"Oh, I didn't realize you had a part-time job."

"Yeah, I work with Mom at the café."

Bob signed the receipt charging the meal to his room, and Glen thought he almost seemed relieved that lunch was over. As Bob walked them to the front door of the hotel, Glen tried to pin his dad down about when they'd be getting together again.

"Well, I can't promise anything right now, Glen. I have to find a place to live, and I'm trying to get the office running smoothly. I hope you understand." Changing the subject, he thrust twenty dollars into Josh's hand. "Here. Don't bother with the subway. Take a cab home and to work. It'll save you some time. The doorman can hail one for you."

"Thanks for lunch, Dad, and the glove. Maybe we can get together again next weekend?" Glen asked hopefully.

"Come on, Glen," Josh said, pulling him away before his dad could answer. "The doorman already has a cab for us."

Glen quickly hugged his dad and ran after Josh.

"You didn't even say good-bye to him," Glen accused Josh as the cab pulled away from the curb.

Josh shrugged. "I don't want to talk about it, Glen."

The brothers turned away from each other, staring out the windows on opposite sides of the back seat.

Arriving at home, Glen climbed out of the cab without a word to Josh. He sat down on the front steps, not in any mood to go in and share how lunch had gone. Just then, the front door opened, and Andrew and Megan stepped outside.

"Glen, when did you get back?" Andrew asked, surprised to see Glen sitting there.

"Oh, just a second ago," he replied, looking at the ground.

Andrew paused, studying Glen for a moment. "Anything you want to talk about?" he inquired carefully.

While Glen and Andrew had both worked hard on their relationship over the past few months, Glen still had some trouble opening up to him. He really didn't want to talk about his dad with Andrew — it just didn't feel right to talk about him behind his back. Maybe if the lunch had gone more smoothly, he would have opened up more.

"Nah, I'm okay," Glen sighed. "My dad got me a pretty cool baseball glove." He handed it to Andrew to look at.

"A Glovesmith, eh? That's great. Maybe we can play catch next weekend," Andrew said, handing the glove back to Glen.

Now why couldn't his dad have said that, Glen thought.

"We're going to the park," Megan piped up. "Do you want to come with us? We could take Jasper, too."

"Sure, Glen, you're welcome to come with us," Andrew added.

"I really should walk Jasper," Glen admitted, "but I think I'll head over to the school yard with him instead. Thanks anyway." Opening the front door, Glen placed the glove on the table just inside, and whistled for the dog. As Andrew and Megan made their way up the street, Jasper bounded happily onto the porch, and Glen took his leash from the hook beside the door.

"Come on, Jasper, let's go play fetch!"

As Glen headed towards the school, his thoughts swirled. Lunch certainly hadn't turned out the way he had hoped it would. He couldn't shake the feeling that his dad was kind of relieved to see them go, and that really hurt. He wondered whether his dad was even glad to be back in Toronto, or whether he had been happier in California. Why couldn't he have invited Glen to lunch again next week? Glen didn't really care what they did, he just wanted to spend time together. He wanted to find a way to get close to his dad again, but he wondered whether that would ever be possible.

4

Making Choices

"That bites. I hate losing," Danny fumed.

The boys had just come off the soccer field and were gathering their backpacks and books. The team had lost their Wednesday afternoon game to the Mustangs, and they were all a little disappointed.

"Guys, one thing before you go," Coach Masotti called. "We will have our next practice on Friday before school, since I'm taking my class on a field trip tomorrow. See you then."

Danny, Glen, and Jacob changed from their cleats into their running shoes.

"You know, if you had just passed me that ball, I could have scored and tied it up," Danny complained to Jacob. "I'm the best striker, after all."

Glen saw Jacob roll his eyes. "You weren't in position! Why would I pass to you when three people were guarding you? I thought Scott had a better chance of scoring."

"But he didn't score, did he? Obviously you thought wrong."

"Stop being such a jerk, Danny." Glen could see that Jacob was getting annoyed. "Sometimes the team's going to lose!"

Danny said something under his breath and stalked off in a huff, leaving Jacob and Glen to walk home together.

"I just can't understand why you put up with that guy," Jacob said, shaking his head.

"He's not bad," Glen protested. "He's a great soccer player, and I get along with him all right. You just need to give him a chance."

"A chance?" Jacob sputtered. "Right from the first day we met him, Danny has either showed off or ignored me or bugged me about stuff. I don't want to hang around with him at all."

"So if I'm doing something with Danny, you're not going to come with us?" Glen asked.

"No, I'm not."

"Come on, Jacob. Danny's the same as any other guy we know."

"No, he's not, Glen. I think he's trouble, and I hope you don't have to find out the hard way."

"Fine." Glen shrugged. "You do what you want."

The boys walked in silence for a while. "Do you want to come back to the school later with Jasper and me?" Glen said finally, trying to break the ice again.

"Well, I have a lot of homework and I have to do some other things," Jacob said, not looking at Glen. "Maybe on the weekend."

The boys parted company at Glen's house, and Glen felt a little upset. He and Jacob hadn't really had a fight, but it seemed as if it might be hard to keep both Danny and Jacob as friends.

After supper, Glen snapped on Jasper's leash and went out into the cool, autumn evening. He still had at least an hour until it was dark, and he headed back to the school yard. Arriving there, he saw Danny playing with a rottweiler.

"Hey, Danny," Glen called. "Is that your dog?"

"Sure is. His name's Magnum. Is that your dog?"

"Yep. This is Jasper. Is it okay to let them play together off leash?" Glen asked. His mother had told him to always check with the owner before he let Jasper play with another dog.

"Yeah, it should be fine," Danny replied, unhooking Magnum's leash. "He's really a gentle dog."

The dogs approached each other, tails wagging, and sniffed each other carefully. After a few seconds, they began to chase each other around the field.

"So, has your dad moved back yet?" Danny asked, taking something from his pocket.

"Yeah, he came back last weekend." Glen was trying to see what was in Danny's hand. "You should see the hotel where he's staying! It's amazing. It has a doorman and everything. We went to lunch in the café and my dad gave me a Glovesmith baseball glove."

Danny shrugged and moved over to the soccer post. "We stay at big hotels all the time when we go on vacation. Maybe you can come with us next time we go somewhere."

Danny had his back to Glen, and Glen could see his arm moving. As Glen walked around to face him, he realized that Danny had a pocket knife and was carving his initials into the soccer post.

Glen watched him, fascinated by Danny's nerve. "Aren't you afraid they're going to know who did that?"

"What do I care? They can't prove it. Lots of people have the same initials. Want me to carve yours here, too?" Danny asked, giving Glen a twisted half-smile.

Glen folded and unfolded Jasper's leash. He didn't want Danny to think he wasn't cool, but he didn't want his initials in the pole either.

"Nah, I did that last year and got into big trouble," Glen lied, biting his lip and turning away from Danny. "The dogs sure are having fun," he said, hoping Danny wouldn't ask him about it.

"Too bad we lost today," Danny said. "I still think I would have scored if Jacob had passed to me. What do you think?" Danny stopped carving and stared at Glen.

"Um, well," Glen stuttered, "you're a really good player, but, um, so is Jacob…" Glen didn't want to give Danny an answer. "Your dad's SUV was really awesome. Was it expensive?"

"Of course it was," Danny sneered.

Glen was starting to feel as if he couldn't say anything right today, and he changed the subject again.

"Where did you go to school before here?" he asked. "How come you guys decided to move?"

Danny looked at Glen in silence for a moment, and Glen shuffled his feet nervously.

"We lived in Scarborough since I was born," Danny finally answered. "But my parents felt I had 'fallen in with the wrong crowd' was how they put it. So they decided to move here, where nothing ever happens."

Glen wondered what Danny meant by the "wrong crowd," but he was afraid to ask.

"Well, um," Glen said, looking around for Jasper. "It's getting kinda late, and I still gotta do my homework, so I think I should head home."

"Wait a sec." Danny grabbed his arm, startling Glen. "It's my thirteenth birthday tomorrow, and my dad said I could invite someone out for lunch. Do you wanna come?"

Glen was supposed to meet Jacob to work on a project, but he really wanted to go with Danny. His mind raced as he tried to think of a way he could accept Danny's offer without hurting Jacob. Glen thought that Danny was cool, and he liked hanging out with him. It made him feel good that Danny had picked him to be his friend.

"I said I'd meet Jacob for lunch. We're doing a science project together—"

"Aw, come on. It's my birthday, and I don't really know anyone else here. Just skip it. If Jacob's such a good friend, he'll understand. Just remember to get a note from your parents to leave school property, and I'll meet you at the front doors at twelve-thirty."

Danny turned away, put two fingers in his mouth, and let out a piercing whistle. Both dogs turned and ran towards the boys.

Clipping Magnum's leash on, he waved quickly to Glen. "See ya tomorrow!" he called, jogging away.

Glen wondered where he was going, since he lived in the opposite direction. He suddenly realized that Danny hadn't really given him a chance to say no, and now he was committed to going to lunch. How was he going to tell Jacob? Danny was so cool, but Jacob was his best friend. He really hoped Jacob would understand. After all, there was still lots of time to get the project done. Attaching Jasper's leash onto his collar, he headed home.

* * *

Walking with Jacob to the soccer practice on Friday morning, Glen felt as if he were talking to himself. Jacob had barely said hello, and it had gone downhill from there.

"And he even let us order double hot fudge sundaes!" Glen looked at Jacob, hoping for a response this time. "With whipped cream and cherries."

"Oh, yeah. Great," Jacob said flatly.

"What is your problem today?" Glen finally asked.

"What's my problem? What's *my* problem? I'll tell you what my problem is — I'm still mad about you taking off for lunch with Danny instead of working on our project. It's due soon, and I feel like I'm doing all the work. You didn't even ask me if I minded! You just told me that you were going."

"Gee, Jacob, relax. We still have a week to work on it. Between this and the way you guys argue on the soccer field, it almost sounds like you're jealous of Danny."

"Jealous!" Jacob said indignantly. "Why should I be jealous of that ball hog? He's not such a great player, Glen. He won't pass to the girls and he plays dirty — I saw him elbow one of the guys on the other team the other day when he thought the coaches weren't watching."

Glen looked at Jacob in surprise. "Are you sure that's what you saw? Maybe Danny was just protecting the ball or something."

"Believe what you want," Jacob fumed. "I know what I saw."

"Come on, Jacob," Glen pleaded. "I'm just trying to make a new friend. After all, I know what it's like when no one wants to talk to you or be your friend. It happened to me in the summer."

"Well, being kind is one thing, but from what I've heard about Danny, he's bad news. I'd watch out if I were you. Look, the rest of the team is ready to go. Hurry up." Jacob ran ahead of Glen, leaving his friend staring after him.

Coach Masotti gathered everyone around to outline how the practice would run today.

"Has anyone seen Danny?" he said, looking around and doing a head count. "He seems to be missing."

"Why don't you ask Glen?" Jacob said sarcastically. "He's Danny's new best friend."

The coach gave Jacob a quizzical look, and Glen felt his face turn red as all eyes turned towards him.

"I don't know where he is," Glen stammered. "I don't keep tabs on him."

The coach looked at the boys in turn and just shook his head. "The first thing we'll try today is the wall pass. Each of you will take a turn with the soccer ball, running along the school wall. You dribble the ball and pass it to the wall. Try to pass it on a forty-five degree angle ahead of you. Then, as it comes back off the wall, you pass it back the same way. I want to see you using the inside of your foot that is farthest from the wall, and the outside of the foot nearest to the wall. We'll try for three passes to begin with."

Standing in line to take his turn, Glen thought about everything Jacob had said. He did have a really good time at lunch with Danny and his dad. Danny had always been nice to him, so Glen decided that he was going to take him at face value. Until something happened to change his mind, he'd hang out with Danny. He decided that Jacob was being ridiculous and blowing things all out of proportion.

Once the entire team had run through the wall-passing drill, the coach had them work on trapping the ball.

"Okay, everyone grab a partner for this one."

Glen turned to Jacob to see him already standing beside Dylan. Glen was rooted to the spot for a moment before Scott came up and slapped him on the back.

"Looks like we're the only ones left," he teased.

Glen smiled sickly at Scott. He couldn't believe that Jacob was being so mean. It just wasn't like him.

"One person in each pair will take the ball and toss it, and I mean *toss* it towards their partner, telling them which part of the body to use to trap the ball. Toss the ball underhand — you're not trying to hurt your partner. If you can easily control the ball from a short distance, increase it slowly. Then switch positions so that you each have a chance at this."

The partners all started the drill, but Glen was having trouble concentrating.

"Come on, Glen. How am I supposed to trap a ball that is over my head?" Scott was getting a little irritated.

"Sorry, man," Glen apologized.

"Another fifteen minutes, then everyone run a quick lap around the school, and we'll call it a day," Coach Masotti instructed.

As the practice was winding down, Danny strolled onto the field.

As soon as he saw Danny, the coach called him over. Glen could hear him quietly reprimanding the boy.

"Gee, Coach, I'm sorry," Danny apologized. "I hate missing practice, but my alarm never went off and I slept in. It won't happen again." Danny looked at the ground and dug his toe in the dirt.

"Well, okay," the coach said. "Thanks for coming and telling me."

As the coach turned away, Danny winked at Glen.

Finishing the drill and running the lap, Glen saw Danny waiting beside his backpack. He and Jacob were both heading over to change their shoes at the same time.

"Hey, Glen, guess what else I got for my birthday?" Danny turned his back to Jacob as he spoke. "I got a mp3 player."

"You know, Danny," Jacob cut in before Glen could respond. "You'll never make the final team by missing practices, and besides, it messes up the whole team when someone is missing."

Danny turned to Jacob. "I don't need to practise like you do," he sneered. "And I'm sure not practising with girls, too. I know I'll make the final team." Danny brushed past Jacob, heading for the school. "Are you coming, Glen?" he called over his shoulder.

"I still gotta put my stuff in my backpack," Glen answered, looking at Jacob. "I'll catch up with you later," Glen called in Danny's direction.

"I'll show him who the star player is," Jacob muttered. "I just don't understand what you're doing being friends with this guy." Jacob stalked away, leaving Glen standing alone.

Watching the retreating back of his best friend, Glen began to wonder if he was going to have to choose between his two friends.

5

Big Surprise

"Hello?" Glen said, answering the phone on the first ring.

"Hey, man," Jacob said. "I'm sure glad we got most of the project finished yesterday. I really feel a lot better now."

The boys had spent most of Saturday at the library and in front of the computer, working on their science project. Glen had hoped that working together would help to ease the tension he had felt between them on Friday, and it seemed to have worked.

"Yeah, me too. It's a load off my mind."

"Want to go inline skating through Thorncliffe Park? This might be the last nice weekend before winter," Jacob joked.

"Don't say that!" Glen exclaimed. "We still have three weeks before the final soccer tournament."

"So, anyway, do you wanna go?"

"I can't right now," Glen said, glancing at his watch. "My mom and Andrew have called some kind of family meeting. I don't know what it's about, but I figure it might have something to do with my dad."

"I wonder what's going on?" Jacob mused.

"I don't know, but I'll tell you later. Say we meet at the corner at three o'clock?" Glen asked. "We should be done by then."

"Okay. See ya later."

"Bye." Glen hung up and headed downstairs.

Throwing himself down on the couch, Glen picked up the converter and started channel surfing. He heard Josh come in the front door, and as his brother sat down, Glen turned off the television.

"Nothing good on?" Josh asked.

"Nah, you know what Sunday afternoons are like." Glen leaned over to his brother. "Do you know why they've called this meeting?" he asked.

"No. I wonder whether something has happened with Dad again," Josh said. "Have you heard from him since we were there last week?"

"No," Glen admitted, looking down at the floor. "I did leave him a message on Friday, but he hasn't called me back yet."

Just then, Megan came bouncing in, ending their conversation. As his six-year-old stepsister chattered on to Josh, Glen thought about his dad again, and about Megan's dad, Andrew. Glen saw all the time that Andrew spent with Megan, and how close the two of them were. He couldn't help feeling a little jealous, not of Megan, but of the relationship between the two of them.

The summer had been a particularly difficult time for both Glen and Andrew as they got used to the new blended family. Since baseball had ended, Andrew had made it a point to include Glen in as many things as possible. That last Blue Jays game he and Andrew had gone to had been the turning point for them. Glen glanced up at the homerun ball he had caught, and smiled, thinking about how out of place it looked on the fireplace mantle, but pleased that Andrew had insisted it go there. Glen knew he should be glad he had such a good stepdad, but he still wished things could be different with his own dad.

His thoughts were interrupted when Catherine and Andrew came in, looking a little worried. They sat down and Andrew asked for their attention.

"We called you guys together this way because it is difficult to get everyone together for dinner these days," Andrew began. "First, I wanted to say that I think it's great that we have all come so far as a family." He looked at the kids in turn and exchanged a smile with Glen.

Catherine was fiddling nervously with her wedding ring. "We do have an announcement to make, and we aren't sure how each of you will react."

Glen felt his stomach drop. Surely now that his dad was living so close to them, they weren't going to move!

"I'm going to have a baby," Catherine blurted out.

The kids sat in stunned silence for a moment as the news sunk in. Josh was the first to break the silence, going over to shake Andrew's hand and give his mom a hug.

"Aren't you getting a little old for this?" he teased, looking down at her. She hugged him back and laughed.

"A baby!" Megan exclaimed. "Do you think I can get a sister? When is it going to come?"

"Well, the baby should be here by March twenty-eighth." Catherine stroked the little girl's curls. "If you do get a little sister, I hope she is as pretty and nice as you are. You're going to be a great big sister."

"Cool! I get to be someone's big sister? That's great!"

Catherine looked over at Glen, who was still rooted to the couch. He couldn't believe his ears. He never imagined he would have to share his mother even further with another brother or sister, especially now, when he was just starting to get close to Andrew. Now Andrew wouldn't have any time for him at all. Glen looked sadly at the baseball once more.

"Glen," Catherine said softly, coming over to sit beside him. "How do you feel about this?"

"Why do you need another kid?" Glen blurted out before he could stop himself. "I just got used to having Megan as a sister."

Megan looked at Glen and promptly burst into tears.

"Oh, Megan!" Glen was horrified that he had hurt Megan's feelings. "I didn't mean it that way. I swear, I didn't mean it in a bad way. I just..." Glen trailed off, hanging his head, as Josh scooped Megan up, hugged her quickly, and gave her to Andrew.

Everyone was talking at once, trying to soothe both Megan and Glen.

"Glen, we don't *need* another child, but sometimes these things happen." Catherine put her arm around Glen's shoulder. "It's a blessing for us."

Settling Megan into a chair, Andrew crouched down in front of Glen.

"Are you afraid that the new baby will take up too much of our time?" he asked.

Glen bit his lip, surprised that Andrew had read his mind. "I guess," he said, trying not to look at Andrew or his mom.

"Well, I won't lie to you," Andrew went on. "The baby will need a lot of attention, but I hope that you will help out as well. We'll still have lots of time together, and this baby really completes our family."

Glen shrugged. It was going to take him some time to get used to this idea. "I'm sorry, Megan. Are you okay?" Glen asked, looking over at Megan still sniffling in the chair.

The little girl nodded. "I'm okay. You do like me though still. Right?" she asked with her lip trembling.

"Of course I do." Glen moved over and sat on the arm of the chair. "I love having you here. I just spoke before I thought. Okay?"

"Okay," Megan said and tried to smile.

Standing up, Glen headed for the stairs to his room.

"Glen, wait!" Catherine called. "I think we need to talk about this some more."

"I can't right now. I told Jacob I would meet him to go inline skating. I gotta go." He ran up the stairs before anyone could say anything else and grabbed his skates out of the closet. Stopping suddenly, he wondered whether his dad knew about this. He listened at the top of the stairs and could hear everyone still talking in the living room. He decided to use the phone in Josh's room and call his dad.

"Hey, Sport," Bob exclaimed. "I was just picking up the phone to call you guys."

"Dad." Glen's voice was a little unsteady. "Are you busy today? Can you come by and pick me up?"

"Why, Glen? What's wrong? I did have a few appointments set up today with the realtor. Is it serious? Can it wait?"

Glen swallowed hard a few times, trying to keep his emotions in check. For some reason, hearing his dad's voice had made him feel worse.

"Mom's pregnant!" Glen burst out.

There was silence on the other end of the line for a few moments. "I see," Bob said quietly. "But it really isn't any of my business, anymore, Glen. Andrew and your mom are married now."

Glen was feeling a little desperate. "Maybe I could come and live with you instead?"

"Glen, you're just upset," Bob said soothingly. "I'm away too much. I work late, and it's just not a good idea. I would have to have someone else stay here with you. It won't be so bad, Sport. You can call me anytime you want—"

"Yeah, fine. Whatever. I gotta go and meet Jacob," Glen cut his dad off and hung up the phone quickly. He grabbed his skates, headed downstairs, and ran out the front door without even saying good-bye to anyone.

The boys had made plans to meet at the Leaside Bridge, but if Glen went there now, he'd be waiting for quite a while. He headed in the other direction, over to Jacob's house instead. Jacob lived on the same street as Glen, but at the other end, in a large bungalow. Jacob had a great big backyard where the boys often played catch in the summer. Climbing the wide stone steps to the front door, Glen rang the doorbell.

Opening the door, Jacob's eyebrows shot up in surprise. "Glen? Am I late? Are my clocks wrong?"

"Nah, I just had to get out of the house. Are you ready to go?"

"Yeah, sure, just let me get my skates and say good-bye to my mom."

Glen paced around in the driveway, waiting for his friend. As soon as Jacob had shut the door, Glen poured out the events of the afternoon to him.

"Wow!" Jacob shook his head. "That really came out of nowhere, didn't it? Soon you guys can field your own soccer team," he joked.

Glen smiled weakly, knowing his friend was just trying to cheer him up.

"You know, it really might not be that bad, Glen." Jacob was an only child, and Glen knew he had always wanted a brother or sister.

"I guess you might be right," Glen sighed. "At least I have six months to get used to the idea. It just took me by surprise."

"Do you really want to go live with your dad?" Jacob asked. "That would mean changing schools, and we wouldn't be able to hang out together much."

"I guess not," Glen admitted. "I was just upset and never thought about what a move would mean. I sort of hung up on my dad, too. I guess I'll have to apologize to him as well."

"Well, Glen," Jacob said, punching him playfully in the shoulder, "that's something you've had a lot of practice at lately!"

6

Toe to Toe

We're doing great, team. The score is tied," Coach Masotti said at the half during Wednesday's game against the Hawks. "And I know you'll win this one. What I need to see though is more teamwork." The coach looked hard at Jacob and Danny. "There seems to be some conflict on the team, and a few of you are playing as if you were the only player out there."

Glen could see Danny smirking, and Jacob was doing everything he could to avoid looking at the coach.

"I'm going to make some changes to the lineup and see if we can shake things up a bit. Glen, you go in for Valerie, and Scott and Dylan, you are in for Jesse and Adam. Salisha, I'll put you in for Dimitri. The rest can stay on for now, and I may make changes as we play."

As the team trotted out onto the field, Coach Masotti quietly asked Jacob and Danny to wait for a moment. Glen tried to walk as slowly as he could to listen to what the coach said.

"I'm leaving the two of you out there for now, because I want you to show me that you can play on the same team. This is not an individual competition. You won't finish this game if this behaviour continues," he warned.

The teams lined up for the kickoff, with the Hawks taking the ball. Making short, crisp, push and flick passes, the

Hawks began moving towards the Tiger goal. Danny tried to tackle the Hawk halfback and take possession of the ball, but the player was too quick for him.

As they passed the centre line, the Hawk player made a passing error, sending the ball directly into Salisha's path. Glen had been playing a shallow defence and quickly ran up to cover Salisha as she headed towards the Hawks net. Seeing a Hawk defender coming in from the side, Glen shouted "Man on!" telling Salisha that a player was approaching and that she should pass the ball quickly.

Glancing up, Salisha made a good pass, but as Glen tried to trap the ball, he deflected it with his toe. Turning to follow the ball in dismay, he was relieved to see that Jacob had been backing him up and now had possession of the ball.

Glen dropped back below the centre line as Jacob took the ball upfield. Scott had manoeuvred into scoring position, and Jacob sent a chip pass flying his way. Scott trapped it easily and quickly shot it hard at the net. The Hawks goalkeeper lunged to the left, stretching out and just barely batting the ball away from the net.

The ball was still live, and the Hawks defender trapped it against his chest. They began passing the ball, pressing towards the Tigers' end, and Glen scrambled back into position with Dylan, Alex, and Sapna, who were playing defence.

Keeping his eye on the ball, Glen waited in the goal area for a chance to either tackle or deflect a shot. As the Hawks' striker drew back her leg to take a shot on goal, Glen stumbled. In a panic to stop the ball, he stuck out his hand and touched it.

Glen drew back his hand in horror as his teammates all groaned, and the Hawks cheered. Touching the ball in the goal area gave the Hawks a penalty kick.

The coach placed the ball about five metres from the centre of the goal. The striker against whom Glen had committed the foul would take a direct free kick from that spot.

Glen held his breath along with everyone else as the striker and the goalkeeper faced each other. Glen had faith in Kaitlynn's abilities, but penalty shots are always difficult to stop.

Mei, the Hawks player who was in Glen's class, took her time getting ready to take the shot, but when she did move, it was like lightning. She fooled Kaitlynn into thinking she was going to shoot to the right, but she sent it into the left bottom corner instead.

The Hawks all jumped up and down, cheering Mei's goal. The Tigers were crestfallen, but they were quick to assure Kaitlynn that she had done her best.

"Don't worry, Katie!" Glen called. "It wasn't your fault!"

At the kickoff, the Tigers took the ball, and the team worked their passes carefully, hoping to come back strong and tie the game. Glen moved upfield with Sapna, leaving Dylan and Alex back to defend, meaning that he was completely out of position, but he found himself with an unusual chance to score. Waving for the ball, he could see Danny out of the corner of his eye, but didn't think he could pass it that far safely. He tried to square his body to the net and kicked the ball hard.

The ball went off his toe rather than the side of his foot, sending it soaring right past the goal and out of bounds. The Hawks would now get a goal kick from the three-metre line.

As the Hawks were getting ready for the goal kick, Coach Masotti called Glen off and sent Valerie in as a sub for him.

"Glen, are you okay?" the coach asked, sitting down beside Glen. "You seem to be having some trouble concentrating. It's not like you to make those kinds of errors."

Glen sighed. "I'm sorry. I guess my mind just isn't on the game today, Coach."

"Is there anything you want to talk about, Glen? You can talk to me, or another teacher, or the school nurse, if you need to." Glen could see the concern on the coach's face.

"No, it's nothing like that," Glen said quickly. "I just have some stuff on my mind."

"Do you just want to watch the rest of the game?" Coach Masotti asked. "There's only a few minutes left anyway."

"Sure." Glen smiled, knowing the coach really didn't want to put him back in anyway.

Watching the game from the sidelines gave Glen a new perspective on the conflict between Jacob and Danny. With a minute left in the game, Glen watched as Danny skillfully dribbled the ball up the field. Jacob was in a prime position to score, and no one was covering him. The whole team was on its feet, yelling for Danny to pass to Jacob. Glen saw Jacob waving at Danny and yelling "I'm open! I'm open!" Glen could see that Jacob had a much better chance to score than Danny, but Danny ignored everyone and took the shot himself. The goalkeeper saw the ball coming all the way and made the save easily. With little time remaining, the Tigers had no more chances to score and lost two to one.

After the teams shook hands, Glen saw Jacob stop Danny in the field, out of Coach Masotti's earshot. Danny was standing with his arms folded tightly across his chest and Jacob was gesturing wildly. The two boys were standing almost toe to toe. Fearing that this might turn into a fist fight, Glen hurried over.

"Why couldn't you just have passed me the ball?" Jacob spat. "I could have scored easily and tied the game!"

"Yeah, right," Danny scoffed. "You wouldn't have scored. What makes you think you could have scored when I couldn't?"

"Because, you idiot—"

"Shut up! I'm not the idiot, you are." Danny glowered at Jacob, balling his hands into fists.

"Guys, come on!" Glen tried to step between the two boys. "It's only a silly house league game. You might not have scored anyway, Jacob. It's done now. Just let it go."

"Whose side are you on?" Jacob asked accusingly. "We're supposed to be best friends."

"Maybe Glen needs a new friend," Danny sneered.

Just then, Coach Masotti stepped in and told them all to get their belongings. "Break it up, boys. The game is over and I won't tolerate any fighting. Get off the field, get your stuff, and go home. You two both better come to practice with a different attitude tomorrow."

Jacob and Danny mumbled their assent and stalked off the field. They gathered their backpacks in silence. Glen saw Danny's dad arrive in the parking lot.

"My dad's here," Danny said, turning to Glen. "Do you want a ride home? Maybe he'll take us for ice cream or something on the way."

"I thought we had already made plans to stop at the doughnut store," Jacob protested.

Glen was torn. Jacob had stood by him through so much, but Danny was so much more exciting. The lure of ice cream was strong. However, looking from Danny to Jacob, Glen told Danny that he'd call him later and turned to leave with Jacob.

"I don't know how much longer I can put up with this guy!" Jacob fumed. "I can't believe we got stuck with him on our team. He's just too much. And you know what Scott told me? It was Danny who pulled the fire alarm the other day at school. You're going to get into trouble if you keep hanging around with that nutcase."

"I think you're exaggerating," Glen said, not really wanting to hear Jacob slam Danny. "Danny likes to have fun, but I'm sure he didn't actually pull the alarm. Maybe he just told

Scott that he did. Everyone seems to have already made up
their minds about Danny, and no one will give him a chance.
Can't you give him a break?"

"Why should I?" Jacob said. Glen could see that Jacob
was getting more irritated. "You are on your own with him,
because I won't be around if Danny is."

Approaching the doughnut store, Glen started fishing in
his pocket for money. "What are you going to get?" he asked,
trying to change the subject.

"I don't feel like having anything now. I'm going home."
Jacob brushed past Glen.

Glen sighed, put his money away, and trailed after his
friend. The boys didn't talk any more on the rest of the walk
home, and by the time he arrived at his house, Glen was
feeling frustrated himself. It was usually Jacob he turned to
when he needed to work through things, and this time Jacob
was too busy being mad at him and Danny to be much help.

He headed upstairs to his room, not really in the mood to
talk to anyone until dinner. He tossed his backpack onto his
desk and went into the bathroom to wash his hands. As he
stepped back into his room, he saw his mom sitting on his bed.

"I think we should talk, Glen," she said, patting the bed
beside her. "You have been hiding out in your room an awful
lot lately. Is there more on your mind than the new baby?"

Glen sat down reluctantly.

"I guess there are a few things," he began, tracing his
finger over the pattern on the comforter. "I'm starting to get
used to the idea of the baby, but I guess I'm just worried. I'm
not sure I'm going to like it, because you and Andrew are
going to be so busy all the time."

"Oh, Glen." Catherine put her arm around him. "You're
right, it *will* be different, and I'll be busy, but I hope you'll
help us with the baby. You'll still be my baby too. You have
been for eleven years and that will never change."

"I guess. I suppose I thought I might have seen Dad more by now, too," Glen admitted. "Even though he's just downtown, he might as well still be in California."

Catherine nodded. "I understand how you feel. Once your dad finds a place to live, I'm sure you can stay with him for the whole weekend. He has to get used to having you so close by, too."

Glen nodded, not trusting himself to speak.

"How is school going?" his mom asked. "Are you enjoying playing soccer this year?"

"School is fine, and I'm having fun at soccer, even if I'm not that great at it. I did make a new friend named Danny."

"Well, that's great!"

"Not really," Glen said. "Jacob doesn't like him, and I feel like I'm stuck in the middle."

Catherine looked surprised. "Jacob doesn't like him? I always thought Jacob was so easygoing. Is Danny new to the school this year?"

"Yeah, he is." Glen was choosing his words carefully, not wanting to tell his mom about Danny's background. "He's in grade six, and he's a striker on our team."

"Well," Catherine said, "judging by the smell in the air, Andrew has dinner ready. How about you come down and set the table for me?"

"Sure," Glen replied, glad that the conversation was over. "I'll be down in a minute."

As his mother walked away, Glen couldn't help feeling a little guilty. He hadn't told his mom everything he had heard about Danny because if he had, she might not let Glen hang around with him. He also had never told her that he talked to his dad after he had found out about the baby, or that he had asked to go live with him. Glen hated not being honest with his mom, but he didn't want to upset her now. He was sure he could handle things on his own.

7

Going Too Far

"Bye, Mom!" Glen yelled. It was Saturday afternoon and he was running out to meet Danny.

"Just a minute," Catherine called him back. "Where are you off to in such a hurry? Are you meeting Jacob?"

"No, Mom. Remember, I asked you last night if I could go to the movies today," Glen said, coming back into the hallway. "I'm going to the Danforth Music Hall with Danny."

"Oh, that's right," his mom nodded. "Is Jacob going too?"

"No, he can't," Glen said quickly.

"All right, but check in with me if you're going anywhere else," his mom reminded him.

"Of course I will," Glen smiled. "Don't I always?"

Glen met up with Danny at the corner of Beechwood and O'Connor, and they walked over to and down Broadview Avenue. The Danforth Music Hall, on the Danforth, had once been a music hall, but it was now a movie theatre that offered special admission prices.

There was a chill in the air, and Glen couldn't help admiring Danny's nice black leather jacket as he pulled the zip up on his own fleece pullover.

As they walked down Broadview, Danny suddenly said, "Hey! I have an idea. Why don't we go downtown instead of going to a movie?"

"Downtown? What are we going to do downtown that we can't do here?" Glen didn't want to admit that he wasn't allowed to go downtown without Josh or a parent.

"Lots of stuff." Danny pushed against Glen's arm with his own. "We could go to the big HMV, or hang out at the Eaton Centre. We could eat at McDonald's or go to one of the arcades. Lots of stuff."

"I don't know if I want to go all the way downtown," Glen hesitated. "I didn't bring much money."

"I have a bank card. I can lend you some," Danny cajoled. "In fact, let's make it my treat."

"Well, um," Glen wavered.

"I know." Danny grinned. "How about we go see your dad? I'd love to meet him."

Glen's heart skipped a beat. He had been dying to go see his dad, but wasn't sure he should do it this way. His mom and Andrew were pretty clear about not going downtown without them.

"What are you scared of?" Danny sneered.

"I'm not scared!" Glen jumped in. "Fine, let's go."

The boys turned into Broadview subway station, and Danny paid the fares. Glen had a knot in his stomach, but he wasn't sure if it was from fear or excitement. They headed down to the westbound platform and hopped on the subway. Once inside, Danny slouched down in his seat, putting his feet up on the pole. Glen could see the irritated looks people sent their way as they tried to get on and off the train.

"Danny," Glen whispered. "Don't you think you should take your feet down? People are having trouble getting past."

"So?" Danny shrugged. "It's a free country."

Luckily it was a short trip to Yonge and Bloor, where they had to change trains. The station was packed, as it always was on a Saturday, and people were hurrying in all directions. Going up the escalator, Danny pushed past people and Glen had no choice but to follow. He didn't want to lose Danny in the chaos.

"Okay, make sure you stick with me and I'll show you something fun at the next station," Danny said, standing right in front of the doors on the southbound train.

As the train drew to a stop and the doors opened, Danny suddenly darted from the train, running alongside it. Glen tore after him, wondering what on earth he was doing. As the warning sounded for the doors closing, Danny leapt into the nearest open door and pulled Glen with him. The door shut on the edge of Glen's sleeve.

"Are you nuts?" Glen panted.

Danny laughed. "Ready to do it again?"

Glen was afraid of being left alone on the train. "Ready."

When the doors opened at the College Street stop, both boys dashed towards the next car. Danny nearly collided with an old lady, but it didn't slow him down. As they hopped into the next car, a transit employee saw them.

"Hey! You two." He pointed at Glen and Danny. "Do that once more and you're off the train."

"Sorry, sir," Glen murmured, his cheeks burning. Danny just smirked.

"We've only got a few stops left anyway," Danny said after the employee had moved away. The rest of the trip was uneventful, and Glen was just as glad.

Coming up the stairs from King Street station, it took Glen a moment to get his bearings. They started to head east along King Street, towards the King Edward Hotel, and Glen soon spotted the doorman.

"There's the King Eddy," he said, nudging Danny and pointing.

The boys walked into the lobby, and Glen stopped.

"Danny," Glen called to Danny, who had kept on walking. "I just realized that I don't know what my dad's room number is."

"So? We'll go ask at the front desk. Haven't you ever been in a hotel?"

Danny got the room number and the boys quickly found the elevators. Glen's stomach was churning, and he was beginning to wonder whether they should have done this. As he was about to tell Danny that he had changed his mind, the doors opened on the fourth floor and Danny stepped out.

They trailed through the hall stopping in front of room 426, and Danny knocked before Glen could say anything.

"Who is it?" Glen heard his dad call from inside.

"Um, Dad?" Glen's voice trembled. "It's me, Glen."

The door suddenly flew open, and Bob stood there with a look of surprise on his face. "Is Josh with you?" he asked, looking past Glen.

"Um, no, this is Danny."

"What on earth are you two doing here by yourselves? I'm sure your mother wouldn't allow this."

Glen shut his eyes for a moment.

"Well, you're here now, so you had better come in." Bob stood aside for the boys to enter.

The hotel room was littered with papers and his dad's laptop was open. Glen could see that they had obviously interrupted him. Bob strode over to the phone, which was lying off the hook.

"Let me call you back." Glen heard his dad say. "Something unavoidable has just come up that I have to take care of. I'll call you back as soon as I can and we'll finish this." The boys stood awkwardly, and Glen felt awful. This had been a really bad idea. As his dad tried to clear some space for the boys to sit down, Danny was inspecting the laptop and trying to read the papers.

"Hey," Bob snapped. "Don't touch that. Glen did you have permission to come down here alone? This is the second time I have asked you."

"Not directly," Glen admitted. "We didn't know we were going to come down here when we left, but I'm sure it's fine."

"I wish you had called first." Bob rubbed his forehead. "I would have set aside some time for you."

"Sorry, Dad." Glen looked at the floor. "I just wanted to see you, but maybe we should just get going."

"Well, I do have to finish that phone call, and get back to work. But listen." Bob reached for his wallet and took out twenty dollars. "I don't want you riding the subway back. Make sure you take a cab."

Walking from the dim hotel interior into the bright sunshine, Glen squinted at Danny.

"My dad's a really busy guy," he began. "He has a very important job, and lots of people rely on him. We could have done something fun if we had let him know we were coming."

Danny shrugged. "Parents are all the same."

Glen took a step towards the doorman to ask him to get a cab, the way Josh had done the last time they were there, and Danny grabbed his arm.

"You aren't really going to spend that money on a cab, are you?"

Glen just looked at him, not sure he wanted to hear what was coming next.

"Let's go to the arcade!" Danny pulled Glen towards Yonge Street.

"I can only stay for another ten minutes," Glen said as they walked up Yonge Street.

He pushed his hands into his pockets, clutching the twenty dollars tightly. The farther north they went, the worse the street began to look. The stores were darker and more run-down. He could hear loud music coming from several doorways, and there were people just hanging around outside of them. Glen nervously stepped closer to Danny. He didn't want to seem uncool, but he was apprehensive.

Reaching the arcade near Gerrard Street, Glen tried to peer in. It seemed to be full of older kids, and Glen could see some of the kids inside had cigarettes, even though a No Smoking sign was posted. He followed Danny inside against his better judgement. It didn't take them long to spend their money, since most of the games took two-dollar coins.

Suddenly Glen heard loud swearing coming from a group of boys at the machines at the back. He could see them starting to push each other, and he began tugging on Danny's sleeve.

"Maybe we should go," Glen suggested.

"Just let me finish this, man," Danny answered, not even turning around.

Glen kept an eye on what was happening at the back, and his heart leapt into his throat when he saw someone pull out a knife.

"Danny, we gotta go right now!" Glen begged. "That guy's got a knife!"

The two combatants faced off, and Glen saw the manager run to the phone. Danny turned to see what was causing all the commotion.

"Come on!" Glen pleaded, pulling Danny away.

"All right, let's get out of here."

The boys took off, running out of the arcade, and headed back down Yonge Street towards the Dundas Street subway station. They raced up to the turnstiles, and they could see the train coming into the station. Glen scrambled to get his change out of his pocket, but Danny ducked around him, jumped the turnstile, and ran onto the train. Glen, scared he would be left behind, fumbled to drop his money into the fare box, and rushed onto the train, too.

Glen could feel the sweat on his forehead, and he clenched his hands tightly. "What is *wrong* with you?"

Danny laughed at him. "Don't be a baby! It was fun. When have you ever had so much excitement in one day?"

"Yeah, well, I don't need that kind of excitement," Glen fumed. "Don't ever ask me to go somewhere like that again. Now my dad's mad at me, too. What a crappy day! We should have just gone to the movies."

"'We should have just gone to the movies,'" Danny mimicked. "I thought you were cooler than that."

The boys turned away from each other, and Glen stared out the window at the blackness.

Glen glanced at his watch. "I'm going to Pape station to take the bus up," he said curtly to Danny. "You can come if you want, but I don't really care."

Glen was never so glad to get home in his life. He closed the front door with a sigh and leaned against it.

"Glen? Is that you?" his mother called from the living room.

Glen jumped guiltily. "Yeah, it's me."

"Can you come in here for a moment, please?"

Glen's heart sank. It was never good news when his mother used that tone of voice.

Catherine and Andrew were sitting on the couch, obviously waiting for him. Glen felt the blood start to pound in his ears as his mother told him that his dad had called.

Glen stood mutely, staring at the floor.

"Just what did you think you were doing? You told me you were going to the movies, and then I get a call telling me you're downtown. Why did you lie to me?"

"I didn't mean to lie!" Glen protested. "I thought we were going to the movies when I left, but then we just ended up downtown."

"You don't just end up downtown," Andrew interjected. "You had to make that decision."

"Why do you smell like smoke?" Catherine demanded. "You're not smoking now, are you?"

"No!" Glen objected. "It's from the—" He stopped abruptly, not wanting to say he had been in an arcade downtown.

"From the what?" Catherine's voice sharpened. "You had better tell me Glen because I'll find out."

Glen swallowed hard. "It's from the arcade," he said quietly.

"The arcade! What were you thinking? No, obviously you weren't thinking. Do you know what kind of trouble you could have gotten into?" Catherine took a deep breath. "We have been sitting here worrying ourselves sick ever since your dad called and you didn't come back right away. He told us he gave you money for a cab."

"I'm sorry, Mom," Glen said, his voice breaking. "I know it was wrong, and I promise I won't do it again."

"Was it Danny's idea?" Andrew asked.

Glen stood silently, biting his lip.

"I guess that answers my question. I don't think you should be hanging around with Danny anymore."

"But—" Glen started to protest.

"No buts," Andrew said firmly. "You're not to see him anymore outside of school, and you're grounded for a week."

"But next weekend is Thanksgiving, and it's a long weekend!" Glen looked at his mother, hoping for support.

"Andrew and I already discussed this, and the punishment is firm. Now, you go take a shower and get rid of the smell of smoke. I have to call your dad back and let him know you're still alive."

Glen ran up the stairs, tears stinging his eyes. He knew he shouldn't have followed Danny, but it had seemed so exciting at first, and he had wanted to see his dad so badly. How was he going to tell Danny he couldn't hang out with him anymore?

8

Heads Up!

"Oh, man! I'm still stuffed from Thanksgiving dinner yesterday!" Jacob stuck out his stomach and patted it.

"I know what you mean," Glen agreed. "And it feels so good to finally be free!" Glen's grounding had meant that he couldn't use the phone, watch television, or hang out after school. His parents had allowed him to attend last week's game against the Sharks since it was immediately after school, and he *had* made a commitment to the team. The Tigers had won three to two.

The boys had just arrived at their Tuesday morning soccer practice.

"It sure is cold this morning," Jacob said, rubbing his hands and blowing into them. "It's just as well the tournament is a week this Saturday. Do you think I have a shot at making it?"

"Of course you do!" Glen said, bouncing up and down to stay warm. "You and Danny are the two players who will make the team for sure."

Glen saw Jacob stiffen at the mention of Danny's name. "Speak of the devil." Jacob nudged Glen and motioned across the field. "Here he comes now."

Glen hadn't seen Danny outside school since he had been grounded, apart from the last game. It had been really difficult for Glen to tell his friend that he wasn't allowed to hang out with him anymore. Danny had been ticked off with Glen and hadn't spoken to him much after that.

"Hey." Danny walked up to Glen and Jacob. "Am I allowed to talk to you here?" he asked sarcastically.

Jacob just turned away, muttering under his breath.

"Yeah, you can," Glen said sheepishly. "Don't be mad at me, Danny. There's nothing I can do. I shouldn't have gone downtown with you."

"Yeah, yeah, whatever." Danny leaned closer to Glen. "There *is* something you can do — you can ignore them."

"Come on, everyone, let's get this show on the road," Coach Masotti called. "Now, I know everyone is still feeling the effects of Thanksgiving dinner, so we will make this a nice, easy practice. After tomorrow's game, the other coaches and I will choose the final twenty-four players to represent the school in the big tournament. We'll post the final list on the gym doors on Friday." The coach looked at each player in turn. "You have all played very well this year, and it will be very hard to pick, but I can only choose four of you. I hope the grade fives will be back to play again next year. All right. Let's get to it."

Glen looked around at all the players. He didn't feel very confident that he would make the final cut. He just wasn't as good at soccer as he was at baseball. Danny and Jacob were obvious choices, but the final two spots could go to almost anyone. Kaitlynn was a great goalkeeper and they would have lost more games if it hadn't been for her, but Dylan was a very versatile player. Then again, Valerie had really improved in the past three weeks. All Glen knew was that he wouldn't get a spot on the team.

As the team was doing its warmup stretches, Coach Masotti began laying skipping ropes end to end in two parallel lines. The team watched curiously. A few feet away, he also set up pylons in a zigzag pattern. Finally, the coach placed three basketballs in a row, about a metre apart from each other.

"For this practice, we are trying something different," Coach Masotti said. "I have set up three stations that will let me see how well you have mastered the different skills. Each of you will have your own ball to work with." Walking over to the skipping ropes, the coach took a soccer ball and dribbled it carefully between the ropes. "The idea here is to keep the ball from touching the ropes. Then, you continue dribbling the ball over to the second station."

The coach moved towards the pylons. "Here, you have to weave through, passing the ball from foot to foot and moving around the pylons." Glen was impressed by the coach's quick footwork. "Last, you come over to the basketballs, and take a shot at each one, trying to hit it softly. Ideally, the soccer ball should come back towards you, but even if you miss, just retrieve the ball and shoot at the next basketball. Then you start the process again. Now, who wants to give a demonstration?"

Danny's hand shot up. "Let me do it, Coach. We did stuff like this at soccer camp all the time."

"All right, Danny, you give it a go."

Danny handled the ball expertly. He flew through all three stations, barely touching the ropes or the pylons, and managed to hit the basketballs in just the right way to send the soccer ball back to him each time.

"Excellent work, Danny," the coach praised. "That's ideally what I would like to see." Glen could see Danny gloating. "However, you all haven't had the opportunity to try this before, so don't expect to do it perfectly the first time. I'm not really looking for perfection, I just want a chance to look at your individual skills."

Coach Masotti divided the team into three groups, and Danny, Jacob and Glen were each in a different group. Glen waited nervously for his turn and watched Danny and Jacob both move through the station with ease. As Adam completed the ropes, Glen moved up to start. Trying hard to keep the ball from touching the ropes, Glen almost lost his balance when he started dribbling. Concentrating on the ropes, he couldn't keep his eye on the ball, and it rolled right over the rope on the left. Glen glanced over to see the coach marking something down, and he hoped the coach hadn't seen that. He quickly recovered the ball, and made his way awkwardly to the end.

Looking ahead, he saw that Adam had already finished the pylon exercise and was waiting to start the shooting drill. Taking a deep breath, Glen lined up with the first pylon. He kept his head down and really concentrated on moving around the bright orange cones, using his right foot to go around the right side and his left foot to go around the left side of the cone. He was surprised when he suddenly found himself at the end of the drill and was pleased he had done so well.

He moved over to the shooting station and really tried to line up his shots. He missed the first basketball entirely, and it threw his confidence a little. He shook it off, and focused on the next target, hitting it cleanly and scooping the ball as it came back to him. Glen managed to hit the final target, but the soccer ball careened off to the right, forcing him to chase it.

The drills continued until everyone had been through them twice.

"That was terrific," Coach Masotti said. "Now, could a few of you help put all this equipment away, and I'll see the rest of you tomorrow for the last house league game."

Glen and Jacob started gathering the skipping ropes, while Danny went to round up the soccer balls. Adam and Dylan began stacking the pylons, and Salisha picked up the basketballs. As Glen and Jacob grabbed their backpacks in one hand and the ropes in the other, they began to walk towards the gym following Coach Masotti.

From behind them, they suddenly heard Danny yell, "Heads up!" Jacob and Glen spun around just in time to see a soccer ball coming at their heads, fast. Glen leapt to the side, but Jacob wasn't quite as fast. The ball smacked the side of Jacob's face, snapping his head to the side and knocking him down.

"What the—" Glen sputtered. "Jacob, are you okay?" He dropped the ropes and his backpack and ran to help Jacob up.

Jacob shook his head. "My ears are ringing," he said, standing up. Glen saw him wince as he rubbed his jaw. He brushed himself off and turned to face Danny, who had jogged over to them.

"Oh, sorry, man. Are you okay?" Danny said without conviction. "I didn't mean to hit you, I was just aiming for the net."

"The net is a metre that way," Jacob snapped, pointing to the left. "You did that on purpose."

"Chill out, Jacob. You're not dead." Danny picked up the ball. "I told you, it was an accident and I said I was sorry."

"You could have broken my jaw," Jacob ranted. "Funny how you can hit a target in practice so easily, but can miss a net by a metre. That was a really stupid thing to do."

"Are you calling me stupid?" Danny asked menacingly.

Glen could see that both boys' tempers were flaring, and he tried to head it off before anything else happened. "I'm sure it was an accident, Jacob." Glen tried to soothe his friend. "I really don't believe that Danny could do something like this intentionally."

Jacob stared at Glen in disbelief, while Danny tried not to smile.

"Is everything okay here?" Coach Masotti asked, having seen the incident. "Jacob, are you all right? I think you should head in to see the nurse. Glen and Danny can finish helping with the equipment."

"Yes, sir," Jacob said, still staring at Danny. "That's probably a good idea." He turned to pick up his backpack.

"Danny," the coach collared him. "I hope that *was* an accident. You could have really hurt Jacob, or Glen for that matter. I hope you apologized to Jacob."

"I did!" Danny exclaimed. "I was just taking a practice shot and it got away from me. I wasn't aiming at Jacob. It really was an accident, wasn't it, Glen?"

"Yes, sir, Mr. Masotti," Glen piped up. "I'm sure it was."

As the coach walked away from the boys, Jacob turned on Glen. "That's it! I have had enough. I won't be hanging around with you anytime you are with Danny."

Jacob stalked off the field and headed to see the school nurse. Danny slung an arm around Glen's shoulder.

"Hey, we don't need him anyway." Danny smiled. "We can have more fun without him."

Glen wasn't so sure. He didn't want to defy his parents, but he didn't want to seem like a chicken in front of Danny either. He figured he could talk to Jacob later and smooth things over.

Glen picked up his bag, and walked into the school with Danny.

* * *

On Friday, kids from all six house league soccer teams were crowded around the gym doors to read the final team list. The coaches had chosen four kids from each team to become the William Burgess Warriors. That team would represent the school at the soccer tournament, where they would play seven other local school teams.

The game yesterday against the Pythons had been a hard-fought battle, and neither team had managed to score. Jacob and Danny had each played very well, but Jacob had tried to stay as far away from Danny as possible. Jacob and Glen had eaten lunch together, but as soon as Danny appeared, Jacob jumped up and left. Glen hated the fact that there was a wedge between him and Jacob now.

"Let me see!" someone said, trying to elbow Glen out of the way. Glen was glad he was a little taller than most of the kids and could read the list from where he was standing. He squinted at it over the other kids' heads and saw that both Jacob and Danny were on the team, and so were Kaitlynn and Dylan. Glen's name wasn't there. He wasn't all that surprised, but he couldn't help feeling a little disappointed. He still intended to go to the final game and cheer on his school.

"Congratulations, Jacob," Glen said, turning to his friend. "You too, Danny."

"Thanks, Glen." Jacob turned his back to Danny. "I'm sorry you didn't make it. We would have had fun together."

"Hey," Danny cut in, tugging at Glen's arm. "I have plans for this weekend that will make you forget all about the team."

"I'm *really* okay with it," Glen protested. "I'm still going to the game to watch you guys. Besides, I can't hang out with you on the weekend. My parents would kill me and I don't want to get grounded again."

"Come on," Danny coaxed. "You can tell them you're going out with someone else."

"I'm not going downtown again."

Danny laughed. "Oh, this is way better."

As Danny walked away, Glen asked Jacob if he wanted to come with them.

Jacob shook his head. "You know you aren't supposed to hang around with Danny. I can't believe you're going somewhere with him, especially when he won't even tell you where he plans to go or anything. If you want to get into real trouble, that's your problem, but I'm not going. No way."

Jacob stalked off, leaving Glen standing alone.

9

Caught!

Glen dragged the rake across the backyard, adding to the pile of colourful leaves beside the tree. He and Andrew were getting a head start on wintering the garden.

"Whew." Andrew drew the back of his hand across his forehead, "that sun is still pretty warm for October."

"I know what you mean," Glen said, shedding his sweatshirt, leaving just a T-shirt underneath. "I hope the weather stays good for soccer next weekend. I would hate to sit in the rain watching the game."

Andrew glanced at Glen. "I'm very proud of the way you're handling not making the final team."

Glen shrugged. "Well, I really joined soccer this year because Jacob wanted to. Baseball is what I like to play." He took a large clear plastic bag and began stuffing leaves into it.

"Here, let me hold that open for you," Andrew said, coming over to help. "How is Jacob these days? I haven't seen him around much."

Glen concentrated on the pile of leaves, avoiding Andrew's eyes. Just then, the phone rang, and Glen jumped.

"I'll get it," Andrew said. "I brought the cordless outside."

Glen was praying it wasn't Danny calling about meeting later. He tried to hear what Andrew was saying, while pretending to be engrossed in raking the leaves. He breathed a sigh of relief when he heard Andrew say his dad's name.

"Glen," Andrew called, "your dad's on the phone." He held the phone out for Glen and retreated to the far side the yard to give Glen some privacy.

"Hey, Sport," Bob greeted his son. "How are things? Did you make the final soccer team?"

Glen was a little disappointed that his dad never called just to see how he was. Bob always called for a specific reason, and it was usually about how well Glen had done or whether he had met a certain goal.

"No, Dad, I'm afraid I didn't."

There was a small pause. "Oh," Bob sounded surprised. "Well, what happened? Did you listen to your coach and try to work on your skills?"

"Yes, Dad. But some kids were just better, that's all. I'm fine with it. But maybe you can come with us to watch the tournament anyway?" Glen asked.

"Well," Bob hesitated. "if you aren't playing, there's really not much point in me coming, is there? I'm pretty tied up with work anyway. We can get together on another day."

Glen wasn't surprised. He hadn't really expected his dad to say yes, but it sure would have been nice. Glen was beginning to see that his dad living in Toronto wasn't going to be much different from his dad living in California.

"I do have some good news," Bob went on. "I finally found a condo to buy. Now you and Josh can come stay for the weekend anytime."

"That's great, Dad." Glen tried to sound excited, but his heart wasn't in it.

"So, shall I call your mom and arrange something for later this month?" Bob asked.

"Sure, I'm looking forward to it."

Glen hung up the phone, feeling a little sad. He wondered whether he'd ever feel close to his dad again.

"Andrew," he called. "Is it okay if I go over to a friend's house to play some video games for a while?" Glen hoped that Andrew wouldn't ask too many questions.

"Sure, but be back for dinner," Andrew replied, putting the rake away and coming over to Glen. "Are you okay?"

Glen knew that Andrew was concerned about the phone call from his dad, so he decided to just let him believe he was upset. It would make it easier to go meet Danny. Still, he couldn't help feeling guilty about hiding things from him, and he slipped his arms around Andrew, giving him a quick hug. He could feel Andrew's eyes on him as he picked up his sweatshirt and left through the gate at the side of the house.

Looking at his watch, he saw he was a little late for meeting Danny, and he jogged up to the corner of Pape and Hopedale.

"Finally!" Danny exclaimed as Glen stopped beside him, panting.

"I just ran all the way," Glen gasped. "I had to be careful, and it wasn't easy getting out without explaining where I was going. Luckily my mom wasn't home, so it was just Andrew. So what are we doing anyway? What's the big secret plan?"

"We're going to build a fort down in the Don Valley." Danny grinned. "It'll be a place we can hang out without anyone knowing what we're doing."

The boys began walking across the Leaside Bridge, and Glen was excited. He had never built a fort before, and he was looking forward to having a special place that only he and Danny knew about.

As they came to the end of the bridge, Glen veered to the left into the ravine, but Danny turned right to cross the street to Overlea Boulevard.

"Where are you going, Danny?"

"What do you think we're going to build the fort with?" Danny asked sarcastically. "We have to get some supplies. We'll head up Overlea."

Glen assumed that Danny was heading to the East York Town Centre and the hardware store and followed him across the street. But as they passed the townhouse construction site near Leaside Park, Danny suddenly pushed aside a loose board in the barrier surrounding the site and ducked in.

"Danny! What are you doing!" Glen exclaimed.

"Quick, come in," Danny replied. "Don't stand there like an idiot. I checked this place out last night and there was nobody here. We'll just *borrow* a few things." He grabbed Glen's arm and yanked him through the opening.

Glen's heart raced. He knew this was trespassing, and they wouldn't just be borrowing—they would be stealing. He stood frozen in place as Danny moved farther away, into a half-finished structure.

"Glen, come on!" Danny stuck his head out of the doorway. "I can't carry all this by myself. Besides, if you help, we'll get out of here faster."

Glen was torn. He could feel a cold sweat breaking out on his back, but he still wanted to build the fort with Danny.

"Can't we just go to the hardware store or to Canadian Tire?" Glen pleaded. "We could buy these things and it wouldn't cost that much. I've got some money with me…" he trailed off, as Danny frowned at him.

"Don't be such a baby! It's Sunday, there's no one around. Just be cool and get in here."

Glen reluctantly followed Danny's lead.

"You grab that wood and a box of nails," Danny ordered, pointing to the back of the building.

The two boys moved to the rear and quickly began picking the things they would need for the fort. Then Glen suddenly stiffened, sure he could hear footsteps. The hairs on the back of his neck rose as he heard a low menacing growl behind them.

Both boys turned around slowly, and Glen went cold all over as he saw a huge German shepherd being held tightly by a burly security guard, who had his nightstick drawn.

"Okay, boys," the guard said gruffly. "Drop the stuff and come with me."

Glen looked around wildly, searching for a way out. But the guard and his dog were blocking the only exit. He and Danny slowly put down the wood and nails they were holding. Glen looked at Danny and saw the other boy's hand shaking. Glen's knees felt weak, but he could see that Danny wasn't going to be much help.

"You know, I should call the police," the guard threatened.

"Oh, please, sir." Glen could feel the tears stinging his eyes. "Please don't call the police. We were just going to build a fort, and we were weren't going to take anything else. We are so sorry! Please, don't call the police," Glen pleaded.

Danny stood mutely, and Glen could see that he was very pale.

"All right, I want you both to follow me, and I'll decide whether or not to call the cops." He moved aside to let the boys out ahead of him. "Just remember that Brutus here runs faster than you do."

Glen bit his lip and sidled past the dog. Danny followed after him and they went with the guard to the security trailer. Inside, the boys sat silently in the stiff wooden chairs, too afraid to say anything else.

"Since you two seem to be sorry for this," the guard said, putting his feet up on his desk, "I'll let you off the hook...this time."

Glen let out the breath he didn't even know he was holding.

"But I'll have to call your parents instead."

Glen's stomach dropped. He wasn't supposed to even be with Danny, much less get caught trespassing and stealing. He gave the guard his home phone number, dreading what Andrew and his mom's reaction would be.

Danny's dad was the first to arrive, and he strode angrily into the trailer. His thick dark hair was slicked back with water, as if he had been interrupted in the middle of his shower. Glen could see that Mr. Jackson's stocky frame was stiff with tension. He clamped a hand onto Danny's shoulder, turning his son to look him in the eye.

"What is wrong with you?" he said through clenched teeth. "Your mother and I give you everything you ask for! We don't understand why you do these things."

"Well maybe you aren't around enough to figure it out," Danny shot back.

Glen saw the tight-lipped expression on Mr. Jackson's face.

"We can discuss this at home. And we can also discuss whether it's time to send you to boarding school."

Glen saw Danny's face fall. He still hadn't said anything to Glen, and he didn't even glance at him as he left the trailer.

As Andrew and Catherine drew up in Catherine's car, Glen could see by their expressions that they were furious. Catherine didn't even get out of the car as Andrew came into the trailer.

"Get in the car," Andrew snapped, his face red with anger. Glen had never seen him like that. "I want to talk to the guard for a moment."

Glen slunk out to the car, with his head down. His mother didn't even look at him. Glen could see her white knuckles as she clutched the steering wheel.

"Mom, I'm sorry," Glen began, the tears trickling down his cheeks.

"Don't," his mother cut him off abruptly. "Don't even talk to me right now. I'm so angry with you, and I don't want to say something I'll regret."

Glen swallowed hard and the tears came faster. He had never heard that tone in his mother's voice before. Then again, he had never done anything this bad before.

Andrew came out and got into the car. They drove home in icy silence. Sitting alone in the back seat, Glen's mind raced. He wondered how he could explain all this. He thought about telling them that he had just ran into Danny on the street, but he quickly dismissed the idea, realizing that lying again would just make it worse.

He wondered what sort of punishment he was going to get, and he felt sick to his stomach. If he was grounded for a week for going downtown, what would he get for breaking the law? His first thought was that he might have to miss the soccer tournament, which meant he would have to explain everything to Jacob.

His head ached as he thought about everything that had happened. If only he could undo the events of the afternoon, he would. Why had he ever gone along with Danny?

10

Clearing the Air

Arriving home, Glen shuffled out of the car, letting his mom and Andrew go in ahead of him, dreading the confrontation that was coming. Andrew and Catherine still hadn't spoken to him. Coming into the house, Glen heard his mother in the living room asking Josh to take Megan upstairs to watch videos. As his older brother brushed past him in the hall, Josh shot Glen a look and shook his head disapprovingly. Glen couldn't meet his brother's eyes.

Turning off the television, Catherine sat down and folded her arms across her chest. "Glen, you might as well get in here now. It won't get any better by standing in the hallway."

Andrew sat down beside Catherine and rubbed her back. Glen crept in and sat down in the armchair, facing his mom and Andrew.

"Glen, what were you thinking?" his mother demanded. "I can't believe you would do something so reckless! Not only did you defy us by going out with Danny, you were caught stealing and trespassing." Catherine's voice was getting higher as she spoke. She leaned her head back against the couch, closed her eyes, and unfolded her arms.

Glen could see that his mother was struggling to control her anger. He felt guilty for lying to his mom and Andrew about Danny, and he felt so stupid for letting Danny talk him into something that he knew was wrong, again. Most of all he felt bad for upsetting his mom so much, especially when she was pregnant.

The tears started to stream down Glen's face, and he wiped them away with his sleeve. "I'm so sorry, Mom. I know it was a stupid thing to do. I know it was wrong, and I know I shouldn't have been with Danny." The words were tumbling out.

"Glen, if you know all these things, then why did you do it?" Andrew asked.

Glen could see the concern on Andrew's face and that he was really trying to understand.

"I don't know why!" Glen blurted out. "I just do things sometimes without thinking."

"Listen, Glen, you have to start taking responsibility for your actions, and more important, you have to think about the consequences of what you do. What if that guard had called the police? What if you had had an accident on that construction site and no one had been there? What then?" Andrew reached over and put a hand on Glen's shoulder. "Glen, you have to trust us enough to tell us what's going on," he pleaded.

"Please, honey," Catherine added. "Why are you behaving this way?" Glen felt as if his heart were breaking. He knew that his mom and Andrew just couldn't fix this for him. Glen had let Danny influence his thinking because Danny did exciting things and somehow filled a void left by Bob.

The words started to pour out. "Dad really hurt me all those times he broke his promises and let me down. I thought having him here would be better, but I think I feel worse. I don't know if he even loves me anymore!" Glen wasn't sure whether he was making any sense, but he couldn't seem to stop now that he had started.

"Danny always wanted to hang out with me and spend time with me. He never said he didn't have time, or didn't want me to come over. I guess he didn't always do the right things, but he really isn't a bad guy. Danny's dad is a lot like mine. He's not around much either, and he thinks that buying presents can make up for it."

Catherine leaned forward and nodded as she listened. "Glen, I do understand, you know. I see the things your dad does, and you're right that he has treated you poorly. But you're wrong if you think he doesn't love you. Your dad's not very good at telling the people in his life that he loves them, and sometimes he isn't very good at showing it either. We both know," she said, including Andrew, "how miserable you were in the summer when your dad didn't show up."

Andrew stood up. "Here, Glen, why don't you sit beside your mother? I'm going to go put the kettle on for tea." He ruffled Glen's hair on his way to the kitchen. "Things are going to get better. We just have to work out some ground rules and make some promises to each other."

Glen sat down beside his mother and hugged her. "It's just that the summer was so hard, and then I was just starting to feel better about our new family. But now everything is changing again with a new baby coming. It's hard enough to share you with Andrew and Megan."

Catherine took a tissue out of her sleeve and began dabbing at Glen's face. "Honey, I know this news has been hard on you. And I know that your dad has really disappointed you, but it's still not an excuse to break the law or lie. There are better ways to cope with situations, and you should have come to us instead, to let us know what you were feeling. You know I've told you already that things will change. But change isn't always a bad thing. We just need to make some adjustments. I'll talk to your dad and try to help him understand how much you need him."

Glen took the tissue from his mom and wiped his nose. He was starting to calm down and took a few deep breaths.

"No matter how crazy it gets around here," Catherine said, putting her arms around Glen, "you and I'll always find time to spend together. We can go for a walk, go to a movie, go to McDonald's, or just sit and talk if that's what you want."

Glen forced himself to smile a little as Andrew came back into the living room with the tea tray. "I think that's a good idea," he said, placing the tray on the table. "And when you're doing something really fun, I want to come too!" he joked. "But in all seriousness, we need to discuss your friendship with Danny."

Glen was feeling very relieved and was ready to promise almost anything. He waited silently to hear what Andrew had to say.

"First, under no circumstances are you to hang around with Danny anymore."

Glen bit his lip. He knew that was coming, but he would miss Danny.

"Second, for at least the next six months, we want you to check in by phone when you're out. If you're going one place, and plans change, you call to ask us whether you can still go. You are going to have to earn our trust again."

Glen nodded. So far he felt that Andrew and his mom were being fair.

"Of course," Catherine broke in, "you're grounded, this time for two weeks with no exceptions."

Glen let a strangled noise escape. "Mom! Does that mean I can't go to watch the final soccer tournament next weekend?"

"Yes, that's what it means."

Glen was devastated. "Mom! Andrew! Please! Jacob is on the final team. I have to be there. He's my best friend. Please, just let me go for that one day and I'll be grounded for another week, or anything you want!"

Glen saw Andrew and his mom exchange a look.

"If we let you go to the soccer tournament, then you will be grounded for an additional two weekends. You will be busy helping Andrew at work doing some yard cleanups and helping me at the café."

"I'll do it," Glen agreed readily. It would be worth it to see that final game.

"Okay, we have a deal then. Now, you head upstairs to your room, and we'll see you for dinner."

"Can I ask one small favour?" Glen asked timidly. "I know I can't see Danny anymore, but can I call him now to tell him that? I want to make sure he's okay, too." Glen bit his thumbnail as he waited for the answer.

Catherine let out a deep sigh. "I suppose I should be glad that you asked permission rather than going behind our backs. You get one phone call."

Glen tore upstairs and into his parents' room to use their phone. He just had to know what happened to Danny after his parents picked him up. Glen was glad that Danny had his own phone in his room so he wouldn't have to talk to his parents.

"Danny, are you okay?" Glen asked as his friend answered on the first ring.

"Yeah, I guess so," he mumbled.

"I got grounded," Glen said. "Did you?"

"Yeah. And I can't even go to that final soccer tournament now."

"But you're playing! Do your parents know that?"

"They don't care." Glen could hear Danny's voice quavering. "They don't care about anything good that I do."

Glen felt sorry for Danny. At least his own parents had understood what was important to him and had let him negotiate his punishment a little.

"Get this," Danny added, "my dad says I'll be going to boarding school after the winter break." Glen heard Danny

sniffling a little. "But I know they'll cave. They always do."
Glen thought that Danny didn't really sound so sure.

"So, um, I also can't hang out with you anymore," Glen
said in a rush. "I wish I could, but I just can't risk it."

"That's okay. I can't hang out with you either."

Glen tried to keep the conversation going, hoping Danny
would apologize for what had happened.

"Look, Glen," Danny finally said. "I gotta go. I have to be
on my best behaviour for a while if I want to get out of this
boarding school thing."

Hanging up the phone, Glen felt a little sad. Danny just
wasn't the person Glen had thought he was. He didn't care
about letting the team down, he only cared about what was
happening to him. Danny didn't seem to be very worried
about Glen either—after all, Glen had had to call him.

Glen walked dejectedly to his room. He was glad to find
Jasper curled up on his bed. The Lab's tail thumped in greet-
ing as Glen went into the room. He lay down on the bed and
snuggled up to Jasper, who immediately rolled over for a
tummy rub. Rubbing his hands through the dog's soft fur,
Glen listened to the murmured voices coming from downstairs.

"Jasper, I almost blew it today. I can't believe I let Danny
talk me into doing something so stupid. I really wanted to be
his friend. He's always seemed so cool and in control, but I
knew deep down that he really needed a friend. I just didn't
think things would turn out this way. I think that maybe
Danny just does bad things so that people will notice him,
including his parents."

Jasper wriggled closer to Glen, his eyes closed contentedly.

"I guess I can understand that Danny wanted his parents to
pay attention to him. My dad hasn't been much better, but at
least I have my mom, and Andrew. I don't think that things

with my dad will ever be the way I want them to be," he sighed. "I guess for now I'm just going to have to get used to it."

Glen rubbed his eyes and closed them, stretching out beside Jasper. The dog flipped over onto his stomach and reached over to lick Glen's cheek.

"At least I know you'll always love me, boy." Glen was actually feeling better than he had in weeks, even though he was grounded.

"At least I get to go to the soccer tournament. And for sure I'm going to stay away from Danny now. Jacob will be glad to hear that — he was right all along, you know. I'm going to have to apologize for everything at school tomorrow. Hey!" Glen's eyes flew open. "I wonder who's going to replace Danny in the tournament now?"

11

Second Chances

The day of the final tournament was cool and crisp, perfect October weather. The sun was shining, and the soccer fields were dotted with players wearing brightly coloured jerseys. The tournament was held at Stan Wadlow Park, which had three soccer fields, and parents and other spectators were sitting along the sidelines in lawn chairs and on blankets.

"Glen, can you pass me a cup of that juice?" Jacob asked, peeling off his track pants. He had his team shorts on underneath, and the final game was starting soon.

"Yeah, sure," Glen said, grabbing two cups and coming over to where Jacob was sitting. "It's been such a great day so far. I didn't think we would get all the way to the finals."

Eight teams were entered in the tournament, and the William Burgess Warriors had already beaten the Cosburn Cougars and the Jackman Jaguars. They would now face the Parkside Panthers for the final game.

"For sure we will at least get a trophy now, even if we come in second." Jacob folded his pants and set them down. "And the best part is, we got to play together after all."

"I know what you mean." Glen couldn't stop smiling. He looked down at the bright red jersey he was wearing and the black shorts with their red stripe. The school crest sat proudly on the left side of his chest, and best of all, his favourite number, thirty-three, stood out in bold black on the back of the jersey. Jacob wore number fifteen.

On Wednesday, Coach Masotti had asked Glen to come to his office after school. The coach had told him that Danny wouldn't be playing in Saturday's tournament after all, and he wondered whether Glen would like to fill in.

Glen had been ecstatic. He ran home that day and asked his mom and Andrew for permission. He kept his fingers crossed the whole way, hoping that since they were letting him go watch, they would let him play instead. After some discussion, they had agreed, and now they were both sitting in lawn chairs with Josh, Megan, and Jacob's parents, watching the boys play.

With the change in lineup, Glen had thought about calling his dad and asking him to come too, but since he had already told Glen that he was busy, Glen decided not to bother. After all, he had the rest of his family there. He waved over at them, and they all waved back.

"Just think what the day would have been like if Danny had been playing," Glen teased his friend. "You never would have touched a ball."

"And if Danny were playing, you'd be sitting in one of those lawn chairs all day," Jacob kidded Glen.

"I know," Glen agreed. "It's kinda funny how things work out." Glen had thought about Danny several times over the past week. He wondered whether Danny's parents were still talking about boarding school.

Coach Masotti jogged over to where the boys were sitting. "All right, guys, we have to get ready for the next game. Just do what you've been doing so far today and we'll do fine. You have both been playing very well."

The boys followed the coach over to where the rest of the team was gathering. Everyone was taking off their track pants and putting their shin pads into their red, knee-high socks.

Everyone had on black soccer shoes with plastic cleats and were holding mouth guards in their hands, waiting to put them in when the game started. Kaitlynn would start the game, and her yellow jersey stood out among the players. She was pulling on her goalkeeper's gloves and had on special padded leggings that would offer some protection on outstretched dives and help to keep her warm when the ball was in the opposing team's end. She was wearing her long black hair pulled back in a scrunchie that matched her jersey.

"I'm really pleased with all the teamwork I've seen today," Coach Masotti said. "No matter whether we win or lose now, you're all winners already. Jacob, I want you out there to start as a striker this game, along with Beatta and Peter. Kaitlynn will be in goal, Torben, Candice, Quentin, and Natasha are defending, and Roger, Claude, and Justin will be our halfbacks. The rest of you will sub in as the game progresses. Now gather 'round for a team cheer!"

The team formed a huddle, and they all placed their hands on top of each other's in the centre of the circle. "G-o-o-o Warriors!" they yelled, pulling their hands out and up over their heads. They heard their fans echo the yell on the sidelines, and the Panthers did the same thing on the other side of the field.

Glen couldn't sit down and kept pacing on the sidelines, watching the action on the field. "Come on, guys," he called cupping his hands around his mouth. "Keep talking to each other out there!"

With so many games to play in one day, they were only playing ten-minute halves. It didn't leave much time to set up complicated plays, so it was important to keep the ball moving as much as possible.

Glen could see that the two teams were fairly evenly matched, but he was pretty sure that the Warriors' fans were louder, clapping and cheering for all the good plays. At the five-minute mark, Glen was on pins and needles, watching as Jacob suddenly found himself in the open, with a clear path to the goal. The Panthers' defenders had let themselves get too far upfield, and their coach was calling for them to get back into position.

Jacob wasted no time dribbling the ball towards the net. The Panthers' goalkeeper was dancing on his toes, trying to anticipate which way the shot would go. He and Jacob each tried to fake the other out, and Jacob finally let a beautiful shot fly at the upper right corner. But the goalkeeper was too quick, and changed direction in mid-jump, putting everything he had into stretching for the ball. He touched it with his hand, and it deflected up first, coming down into his out-stretched palms. He pulled it into his chest as he hit the ground and rolled, holding it until the whistle sounded.

"Good shot, Jacob!" Glen called from the sidelines, adding his voice to those of the spectators. "I really thought you had that one!" He clapped his hands and whistled a few times.

The defence was playing really well on both sides and the teams were scoreless at the half. Coach Masotti was very upbeat and pleased with the way the game was going.

"Just remember, everyone, the most dangerous player on the field is the one in possession of the ball. You have to cover your opposing player. I know you can win this game, as long as you keep playing as a team. Now, we'll let the other players give it a shot. Jacob and Kaitlynn, you stay in. Glen, Dylan, Abdul, and Quan will be the defenders, Devon and Anthony, you join Jacob as strikers, and Avivah, Madhu, and Samantha will be halfbacks."

After the kickoff the Panthers took immediate possession of the ball and scampered down the field, straight at Quan and Abdul. The Panthers' striker easily dodged Quan's tackle, and Abdul was just a bit too far away to help. The ball streaked straight into the net, before Kaitlynn even had time to react. The Panthers' players exploded into cheers and jumped around high-fiving each other. Their fans were on their feet, clapping and hollering. On the Warriors' side, everyone was calling encouragement and telling them to shake it off. It was only one goal.

The goal seemed to set something on fire in Jacob. Everywhere Glen looked, Jacob was making a play, or just keeping everyone's spirits up. He was always on the move, tracking the ball like a bloodhound.

As the Warriors took possession of the ball again, Jacob headed the charge upfield. "Jacob!" Devon yelled. "Over here! I'm open, Jacob!"

Glen watched, holding his breath as Jacob sent the pass ripping towards Devon. She trapped it easily and kept going towards the net. Glen watched her feet flying and was impressed that she could keep the ball so well under control. As she neared the goal, the rest of the team were on their feet, chanting, "Devon! Devon!"

Glen's hands were clenched and he could hardly breathe from the excitement. Devon's excellent footwork fooled the goalie into going left while she went right, putting the ball in the net. The game was tied!

Everyone on the Warriors' team mobbed Devon, slapping her on the back and congratulating her on the tying goal. Glen was more determined than ever to win.

The play went back and forth for the next few minutes, with the Warriors looking for a way to break through, and the Panthers struggling to recover from the goal. Glen could see that it had really shaken their confidence.

The referee signed two minutes to play, and the Warriors turned up the heat on the other team. Glen stayed close to his opposing player. When she got the ball, he quickly looked to see where the other defenders were, and saw they were covering him. He decided to go for the tackle since they could get the ball if he missed.

Glen challenged the Panther, staying between the attacker and his home net. Keeping his movements tight and controlled, Glen came in quickly, forcing the other player away from the net. Glen concentrated on the ball. Stepping in close and using his foot to make contact, he knocked it loose. He protected the ball by turning his shoulder to the Panther and gained possession.

Glen's stomach was doing flip-flops. That was the first time he had ever tackled successfully. He dribbled up the field, and spotted Jacob running ahead of him.

"Heads up, Jacob!" Glen called. He used the laces to send the ball over everyone's head. Jacob jumped, trapping the ball high on his chest, and let it drop lightly to the ground, keeping his hands well away from the ball.

Glen kept running up the field. He had to be close to watch Jacob take this shot. Glen's pass had given Jacob some room to manoeuvre, with most of the Panthers still running. Jacob tore up the field, and all the parents and spectators were on their feet, urging him on. Coach Masotti was yelling instructions, and Glen couldn't even speak.

Staring straight at the goalkeeper, Jacob drew his leg back and kicked the ball as hard and as high as he could. Glen felt the world stop turning as the ball hit the crossbar with a resounding thud.

The ball ricocheted straight back at Jacob. Glen saw Jacob react fast and kick the ball to the side of the goal. The Panthers' goalkeeper had leaped to stop the first kick and couldn't recover fast enough. The ball sailed into the net, unobstructed.

Jacob had scored the go-ahead goal!

The referee had a hard time bringing everyone under control for the kickoff again.

Glen could feel the adrenaline pumping through his system. They just had to hang on for less than a minute to win the game.

"Everyone play defensively!" Coach Masotti yelled. "We're already ahead and don't need to score again."

The Warriors never even let the Panthers near the net.

With the final blast of the whistle, the Warriors burst onto the field, with everyone hugging and clapping and yelling. The Warriors had won the tournament! The two teams lined up to shake hands. The Panthers showed themselves to be good sports.

"Gather 'round one last time," Coach Masotti called to the team. "I want you to choose the MVP now." He handed out pieces of paper and pencils to everyone. "Now, think back over the three games we played today and choose someone as the most valuable player. It may not be the person who scored the most, or saved the most, but the person whose energy and enthusiasm kept our confidence alive when we were down."

Everyone took a few moments to think about their choice and then handed the ballots back to the coach. He quickly noted their choices on his clipboard.

"I'm pleased to announce that the MVP for the area-wide tournament this year is..." Coach Masotti paused, drawing out the suspense. "Jacob Collins!"

Everyone applauded Jacob, and the coach shook his hand. "Good work, Jacob. I really think you deserve it," he said smiling. "The trophies will all be handed out at next week's school assembly."

Glen slapped Jacob on the back. "Congratulations, man! I voted for ya. You really were great to watch out there."

The whole team gathered around, and they did one final cheer, with Jacob in the middle.

Glen and Jacob high-fived each other one more time.

"We better get our stuff together," Glen said. "Everyone looks anxious to congratulate us, and they haven't even heard that you won MVP yet!"

The boys quickly gathered their bags and ran over to their families, grinning at each other.

* * *

Three weeks later, Glen and Jacob ran into Danny at the mall. It was the first time Glen had seen Danny outside school since they had been caught on the construction site. Glen had done his best to avoid Danny at lunch and after class, and he hadn't really spoken to him since that final phone call. But it was difficult to walk past him now without saying anything.

"Hey, Danny." Glen stopped and put down the bag he was carrying. "How's it going?"

"Not bad," Danny replied. "I'm surprised you stopped. I thought you weren't allowed to talk to me anymore."

"Well, I can't hang out with you, but it's not like I hate you or anything."

Jacob shook his head. "I'll be waiting for you over there, Glen," he said, walking away and sitting on a bench.

Danny snorted. "I see Jacob likes me as much as ever."

Glen shrugged. "So what ever happened about boarding school? Are you still going after the winter break?"

Danny laughed. "Boarding school? Nah, I told you my parents would cave. I just had to behave myself for a while and promise to be a good boy." His voice was full of sarcasm.

"Are things any different with your parents?" Glen knew that Danny was lonely at home and needed his parents' attention, even if he didn't want to admit it.

"Aw, some things never change." Danny didn't meet Glen's eyes. "But I don't care. At least I always get my own way. Hey look!" he said, pointing to the end of the mall.

"There's an arcade!" Danny rubbed his hands together gleefully. "Wanna check it out?"

Glen sighed and saw Jacob's head whip around in the direction that Danny was pointing. "You're not serious, are you?" Glen asked.

Striding over to them, Jacob grabbed Glen's arm. "Don't even think about it," he warned.

Glen laughed. "Don't worry! I wasn't going anywhere. Look, Danny," Glen said turning to him again. "You know I can't go with you. I'm sorry things turned out the way they did, but this is the way it's gotta be."

Danny grinned at Glen, arching one eyebrow. "I know. But I just thought I'd try. See ya around!" He brushed past Jacob and sauntered off in the direction of the arcade.

Reaching out an arm to steady his friend, Glen stared at Danny's back as he walked away. "You know what?" he said, shaking his head. "For once Danny's right. Some things never change."

Other books you'll enjoy in the Sports Stories series ...

Baseball

☐ *Curve Ball* by John Danakas #1
Tom Poulos is looking forward to a summer of baseball in Toronto until his mother puts him on a plane to Winnipeg.

☐ *Baseball Crazy* by Martyn Godfrey #10
Rob Carter wins an all-expenses-paid chance to be batboy at the Blue Jays spring training camp in Florida.

☐ *Shark Attack* by Judi Peers #25
The East City Sharks have a good chance of winning the county championship until their arch rivals get a tough new pitcher.

☐ *Hit and Run* by Dawn Hunter and Karen Hunter #35
Glen Thomson is a talented pitcher, but as his ego inflates, team morale plummets. Will he learn from being benched for losing his temper?

Basketball

☐ *Fast Break* by Michael Coldwell #8
Moving from Toronto to small-town Nova Scotia was rough, but when Jeff makes the school basketball team he thinks things are looking up.

☐ *Camp All-Star* by Michael Coldwell #12
In this insider's view of a basketball camp, Jeff Lang encounters some unexpected challenges.

☐ *Nothing but Net* by Michael Coldwell #18
The Cape Breton Grizzly Bears prepare for an out-of-town basketball tournament they're sure to lose.

☐ *Slam Dunk* by Steven Barwin and Gabriel David Tick #23
In this sequel to *Roller Hockey Blues*, Mason Ashbury's basketball team adjusts to the arrival of some new players: girls.

☐ *Hockey Night in Transcona* by John Danakas #7
Cody Powell gets promoted to the Transcona Sharks first line, bumping out the coach's son who's not happy with the change.

☐ *Face Off* by C.A. Forsyth #13
A talented hockey player finds himself competing with his best friend for a spot on a select team.

☐ *Hat Trick* by Jacqueline Guest #20
The only girl on an all-boys' hockey team works to earn the captain's respect and her mother's approval.

☐ *Hockey Heroes* by John Danakas #22
A left-winger on the thirteen-year-old Transcona Sharks adjusts to a new best friend and his mom's boyfriend.

☐ *Hockey Heat Wave* by C.A. Forsyth #27
In this sequel to *Face Off*, Zack and Mitch encounter some trouble when it looks like only one of them will make the select team at hockey camp.

☐ *Shoot to Score* by Sandra Richmond #31
Playing defence on the B list alongside the coach's mean-spirited son is a tough obstacle for Steven to overcome, but he perseveres and changes his luck.

☐ *Brothers on Ice* by John Danakas #41
Brothers Troy and Trent both want to play goal for the same team.

☐ *Rookie Season* by Jacqueline Guest #42
What happens when a boy wants to join an all-girl hockey team?

☐ *Brothers on Ice* by John Danakas #44
Tempers flare when two brothers both try out for the position of goalie on their community club team.

Riding

☐ *A Way With Horses* by Peter McPhee #11
A young Alberta rider invited to study show jumping at a posh local riding school uncovers a secret.

☐ *Riding Scared* by Marion Crook #15
A reluctant new rider struggles to overcome her fear of horses.

☐ *Katie's Midnight Ride* by C.A. Forsyth #16
An ambitious barrel racer finds herself without a horse weeks before her biggest rodeo.

☐ *Glory Ride* by Tamara L. Williams #21
Chloe Anderson fights memories of a tragic fall for a place on the Ontario Young Riders' Team.

☐ *Cutting it Close* by Marion Crook #24
In this novel about barrel racing, a talented young rider finds her horse is in trouble just as she is about to compete in an important event.

☐ *Shadow Ride* by Tamara L. Williams #37
Bronwen has to choose between competing aggressively for herself or helping out a teammate.

Roller Hockey

☐ *Roller Hockey Blues* by Steven Barwin and Gabriel David Tick #17
Mason Ashbury faces a summer of boredom until he makes the roller-hockey team.

Running

☐ *Fast Finish* by Bill Swan #30
Noah is a promising young runner headed for the provincial finals when he suddenly decides to withdraw from the event.

Sailing

☐ *Sink or Swim* by William Pasnak #5
Dario can barely manage the dog paddle, but thanks to his mother he's spending the summer at a water sports camp.

Soccer

☐ *Lizzie's Soccer Showdown* by John Danakas #3
When Lizzie asks why the boys and girls can't play together, she finds herself the new captain of the soccer team.

☐ *Alecia's Challenge* by Sandra Diersch #32
Thirteen-year-old Alecia has to cope with a new school, a new stepfather and friends who have suddenly discovered the opposite sex.

☐ *Shut-Out!* by Camilla Reghelini Rivers #39
David wants to play soccer more than anything, but will the new coach let him?

☐ *Offside!* by Sandra Diersh #43
Alecia has to confront a new girl who drives her fellow teammates crazy.

☐ *Heads Up!* by Dawn Hunter and Karen Hunter #45
Do the Tigers really need a new, hot-shot player who skips practice?

Swimming

☐ *Water Fight!* by Michele Martin Bossley #14
Josie's perfect sister is driving her crazy but when she takes up swimming — Josie's sport — it's too much to take.

☐ *Taking a Dive* by Michele Martin Bossley #19
Josie holds the provincial record for the butterfly, but in this sequel to *Water Fight,* she can't seem to match her own time and might not go on to the nationals.

☐ *Great Lengths* by Sandra Diersch #26
Fourteen-year-old Jessie decides to find out whether the rumours about a new swimmer at her Vancouver club are true.

Track and Field

☐ *Mikayla's Victory* by Cynthia Bates #29
Mikayla must compete against her friend if she wants to represent her school at an important track event.